W.H.G. Kingston

The Young Berringtons

The Boy Explorers

W.H.G. Kingston

The Young Berringtons
The Boy Explorers

ISBN/EAN: 9783337416706

Printed in Europe, USA, Canada, Australia, Japan

Cover: Foto ©Raphael Reischuk / pixelio.de

More available books at **www.hansebooks.com**

THE

YOUNG BERRINGTONS:

OR, THE BOY EXPLORERS.

BY

W. H. G. KINGSTON,

AUTHOR OF "OVER THE ROCKY MOUNTAINS," "AT THE SOUTH POLE,"
ETC., ETC.

CASSELL, PETTER, GALPIN & CO.,

LONDON, PARIS & NEW YORK.

This Story originally appeared in a volume of *Little Folks*, now out of print.

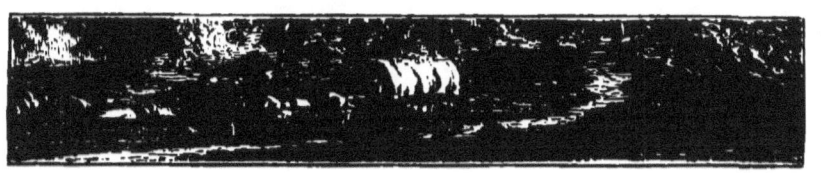

CONTENTS.

"A BLACK FIGURE STARTED UP, AND HURLED A LONG LANCE AT HIM" (*p.* 8).

THE
YOUNG BERRINGTONS:

Or, THE BOY EXPLORERS.

CHAPTER I.

The Young Colonists Introduced—Expectant Relatives—In Search of
" Old Bolter "—A Dinner in the Bush—Bolter tries to Escape—Encounter Blacks—Bolter brought back—Sandy Macdougal.

 " I WONDER what sort of fellows
these English cousins of ours
will turn out ? " exclaimed Harry
Berrington, as he rode up alongside
his elder brother Paul. " Judging by
their photographs, which Uncle
Frank sent us out last year, I have
an idea that they are mighty fine
young gentlemen, who will be apt to turn up their noses
at us colonial ' corn-stalks.' "

" Hector and Reginald are good-looking fellows, I
should think, and wear fine clothes · but beyond that—

whether they are dark or fair, have blue eyes and pink cheeks, or whether they can ride, and shoot, swim, and play cricket, or can only dance and sing, or draw, or such-like girlish things—I have not the slightest notion," answered Paul. "We shall, however, soon know; for, according to the letter father got yesterday their ship ought to reach Moreton Bay in the course of three or four weeks; and I hope that I may have the chance of going down to Ipswich to meet them."

"I don't think you will be so lucky," observed Harry. "I heard father say that he intended going himself, as he expected poor Aunt Augusta would require a good deal of attention, as she has been accustomed to live luxuri-ously, and has never done anything for herself. From a remark he made, I suspect that both the boys and girls have been brought up in the same fashion. Although they may get into our ways at last, they won't like our style of life at all when they first arrive."

"They must learn to like it, somehow or other," observed Paul. "Poor Uncle Frank! I really pity him; he has lost nearly all his fortune; and to be obliged, at his time of life, to begin to work hard! And work hard he must, like the rest of us."

"Yes, indeed; I have heard mother say that they lived in a large house in London, with butlers, footmen, housekeeper, nurses, and all sorts of servants; and had carriages and horses, and saw lots of company," said Harry.

"They'll not have much of that out here; they will have to be their own servants, or consider themselves for-tunate if they can hire an Irish girl, or get a black *gin* to do the rough work. We must try and help them, how-ever, as much as we can, until they get accustomed to our ways," observed Paul. "And Mary, and Janet, and Lizzie will, I am sure, do their best to save them trouble."

"Of course, we all will, in reality; but I don't think I shall be able to help laughing when I see the exquisite Mr. Hector and his brother Reginald attempting to round up cattle, riding after stray horses, or milking cows. And there are two other boys—Edgar and Albert. I wonder what they will be like; they are about the same ages as Rob and Tommy, and if they are as great pickles they will manage to lead each other into all manner of scrapes; but we shall have rare fun with the girls if they have got any life in them."

The two speakers were fine, active-looking lads, sons of Captain Hugh Berrington, who had settled in the colony of Queensland a short time before Paul, the eldest, was born. They might have been known as young gentlemen by the tone of their voices rather than by their costume, which consisted of a red serge shirt, loose trousers fastened at the waist with a leathern belt, large boots coming up to their knees, and broad-brimmed cabbage-tree hats. Each carried in his hand a heavy whip with a long thick thong. The elder, in addition, had a brace of pistols in his belt, which weapons were necessary in case of the sudden appearance of any strange natives. They were mounted on strong, active little horses, which evidently got but a small amount of grooming.

The lads had just left their home, which was situated on the banks of the Burnett river. It is worthy of a short description. The house, though built entirely of wood, and on one floor, was a substantial-looking building, containing ten rooms, with a broad verandah running entirely round it. The frame-work was of rough timber, and the walls were composed of slabs, which are boards split out of the iron-bark or blue gum-tree. The roof was covered with shingles, or tiles of wood, split like the slabs and sawn to the required size.

Round the homestead was a field of Indian corn, an

orchard full of fruit-trees of various descriptions, a kitchen garden supplying all sorts of vegetables, and a smaller space devoted to flowers, most of which would have been highly prized in an English conservatory. There were several out-buildings beyond the cultivated ground, with yards and pens for cattle and sheep.

Altogether, Stratton was considered a very flourishing little homestead, of which the owner was justly proud. The sun had scarcely risen, when, after a hurried break-fast, the two young Berringtons had set out on an expedition in search of "Old Bolter," one of their horses, well so-called, who—no unusual circumstance—was reported missing. They had a difficult task before them, for Old Bolter was a cunning rogue, and by this time had probably got far away into the bush; but to find him they were determined, as he was wanted for work, and could do twice as much as any other horse when he chose. They were now, as fast as the numerous trees would allow them, cantering forward through a scrub, extending for some distance from the banks of the river. Familiar as was the scenery to them, Paul, who had an eye for the picturesque, could not help remarking the beauty of the rich tropical vegetation amid which they were passing. The sun, now rapidly rising behind their backs, threw a bright glow on the dark-green branches of the huge fig-trees, the feathery leaves of the cabbage and other palms, and here and there, tall pines or red cedars, towering above the mass of foliage, with vines and creepers of many hues hanging to the boughs in wreaths and festoons, or extending to the ground like loose ropes from the rigging of a ship.

They soon got clear of the scrub, for Old Bolter would certainly not be hiding within it, for the best of reasons— not a blade of grass grew on the leaf-covered ground. They now entered the more open country, called forest land, in contradistinction to the scrub. Here, though gum-trees of vast size towered to the sky, they generally stood far apart—their curiously-shaped leaves, with their edges turned upwards, allowing the sun's rays to penetrate to the grass-covered ground.   Paul and Harry now began to look out eagerly for the runaway.   There were one or two places in which he had before been found, and these they had settled first to visit.   They were gullies, or dry creeks, bordered thickly by trees, beneath the shade of which he could stand during the heat of the day, and, while whisking off the flies with his long tail, meditate at his leisure.   Three of these places were visited, but Old Bolter was not there.   The water-holes in their neighbourhood were dry, which would account for the absence of the knowing old steed.

"He has gone to Myall Creek, depend upon it," observed Paul; "we shall find him in the scrub thereabouts."

Harry agreed that his brother was very likely correct in his surmise, and, the ground being open, they again rode forward.   Harry especially delighted in a hard gallop.   By getting over the ground at an early hour, they might rest during the heat of the day under the shade of the myall trees—from which the creek took its name—and employ themselves in shaping a few stock whip-handles, which are made from its fragrant wood ; they would then recommence their search for Old Bolter.   Once having found him, there would be no stopping until they had got him safe back into the paddock.   An hour's hard riding brought them up to Myall Creek, within the dry bed of which they hoped to find Bolter, provided he had not discovered their approach, when to a certainty he would be off to some other place of concealment.   They had prudently brought provisions with them, and, having securely hobbled their horses so that they might feed close to them, they sat down beneath the shade of a tree on the edge of the scrub and ate their dinners. They then cut some sticks from the myall trees suited for their purpose, and, while they sat resting in the shade, employed themselves in shaping the wood into the required size with their knives.

"Now," cried Paul, jumping up, "we must hunt up Old Bolter."

RESTING ON THE EDGE OF THE SCRUB.

They quickly caught their steeds, and unhobbling them mounted.

"You go round the north side, and I will take the south of the bush," said Paul. "If you see Bolter, cooey to me, and take care that he does not make off westward, or we shan't get back to-night—or to-morrow, perhaps."

"No fear about that. I'll head him if I catch sight of

his ears, and take good care to turn him towards you."

Harry accordingly rode away to the northward, while Paul directed his course round the southern end of the bush, and then circling round, reached the west side of the creek, in the dry bed of which he hoped to find Bolter. He examined the ground carefully, expecting to find some track of the missing horse, but not a sign could he see. Half an hour or more elapsed, when he heard Harry's shrill cooey ; but, from the faintness of the sound, he knew that his brother must be a long way off. Putting spurs to his horse he galloped forward, expecting every moment to see Bolter dash out of the creek and make for the west. At last he caught sight of Harry, and directly afterwards, from some thick bushes, out sprang Bolter, and, as had been expected, made off towards the west, just midway between the two lads.

"After him ! " cried Paul, and turning their horses' heads they gave them the rein. The animals seemed to know the object of the chase, and were eager as their riders to overtake the truant.

The ground was rough and broken, with here and there trees lying across it, blown down by a whirlwind ; but they scarcely stopped Bolter, who seemed to take an especial pleasure in leaping over them, and leading his pursuers along the worst ground he could find. The other animals were, however, quite as eager to come up with Bolter as he was to escape, and exerted themselves to the utmost. Should he once get out of sight, as there appeared every probability of his doing, days might pass before he could again be discovered. They were approaching another scrub, which was, however, sufficiently open to allow the horses to pass through.

"If he once gets in there, our game will be up ! " cried

Paul. "On, Harry, on! we must head him before he reaches it."

"Very well to sing out, 'On, on!' My beast is doing his best, and Bolter doesn't intend to be caught," cried Harry.

That Bolter would escape seemed very likely. He had got within a few yards of the scrub, when he suddenly wheeled round, almost on his haunches, and galloped back the way he had come. Scarcely had he done so, when a black figure started up from behind some bushes, and hurled a long lance at him, but the weapon merely grazed his side, and stuck in the ground.

"Back, back! the blacks! There may be more of them!" cried Paul.

Harry had seen the native, and pulled up as his brother spoke. They were just in time, for a dozen or more black fellows, showing themselves, sprang forward poising their spears ready to hurl at the young horsemen. Old Bolter, fully comprehending the danger which he and his owners were in, instead of going over the bad ground took that to the left, allowing Paul and Harry to ride up close to him on either flank. Nevertheless, he kept his eyes about him, evidently intending to make off in some other direction if he could. The three horses now tore along over the ground, the nimble-footed blacks, with their spears in hand, following them for some distance. At length, however, Paul, looking back, found that they had got well ahead of the natives. It was important not to be overtaken, for they evidently belonged to some hostile tribe who intended mischief. Bolter, who seemed to be aware that there was no longer any danger from the blacks, made two or three attempts to escape; but Paul and Harry reminding him of his duty with their stock whips, he at length made straight as an arrow for the station, over the very course they would have chosen.

Nothing stopped him. Across the country he galloped, with the two riders on either side. As they approached the yard they shouted to Sandy Macdougal, the overseer, who, fortunately, was close at hand, to open the gate, and in rushed Old Bolter.

"We had a hard matter to find him, and he would have got away from us after all if a number of black fellows had not tried to spear him," observed Paul. "We must be on our guard against them, or they will be doing some mischief."

"You've indeed done vera weel to bring the brute back so soon," said Sandy, as he carefully closed the gate, not to give Bolter another chance of escaping. "It would be wise to send over to Ogilvie to let the police know that there are strange blacks in the neighbourhood. Better to prevent the mischief than punish their puir bodies after it's committed, and as they attacked you, there's sufficient reason for warning them to take their departure."

The lads having unsaddled their horses, turned them into the paddock, and, accompanied by Sandy, repaired to the house. On the way the overseer inquired more particularly about their meeting with the blacks.

"It's a mercy they did na spear you. Praise the Lord for His goodness, lads; He always watches over those who trust Him. Dinna fail to do that."

Sandy Macdougal was an old follower of Captain Berrington. He had accompanied him from ship to ship as his coxswain; and when the captain retired from the service, and obtained the allotment of land on which he finally settled in Australia, Sandy, though he might have obtained a pension by serving a year or two longer at sea, insisted on accompanying him. While the captain was going through the arduous work of settling, Sandy was like his right hand. When the old sailor might have set up a farm of his own he declined doing so, preferring to serve his old commander in the capacity of overseer; and most faithfully did he discharge his trust.

CHAPTER II.

THE drays for the in-
tended journey were
packed, and the horses put
to. The captain stood
ready, booted and spurred.
Harry, to his great de-
light, was to accompany
his father. Paul would
much have liked to go,
but not the slightest sign
of disappointment did he
allow himself to exhibit;
indeed, he was justly proud
of having the responsibility, with the aid of Sandy, of
looking after the family.

The drays were not at all like the cumbersome vehicles
which are known under that name in England. They
were merely large, strongly-built carts on two wheels,
drawn by three, four, or five horses, as the nature of the
country might require; though, on a smooth road, one
could drag them. Old Bolter might have suspected that

he would be wanted when he ran off, for he was put into the heaviest. They were now chiefly loaded with wool and other produce, and with a few articles the travellers required for their journey. On the return journey they would be fitted in a very different way—with canvas tilts to keep out the sun or rain, while in the inside goods were to be packed, easy chairs, or piles of bedding, and cushions for the accommodation of the ladies and young children. Besides the horses for the drays, four others were taken, in case the new arrivals should wish to ride. They were steady animals, not addicted to following Old Bolter's example. The drays having been sent on ahead, the captain and Harry, wishing the loved ones at Stratton good-bye, mounted their horses, and quickly overtook them. The captain felt no anxiety about the blacks, as Sandy had given notice to the police of their threatened attack on the young Berringtons, and a party had been sent out, under an experienced officer, to drive them away.

Now that her husband was fairly off to meet his brother's family, Mrs. Hugh Berrington began to realize the fact that they were coming, and actively commenced making preparations for their reception. She was a motherly, active, cheerful little woman, who never, by any chance, lost her temper, even under the most vexatious circumstances, and always saw things on the bright side.

Her girls were very like her in many respects—hearty, merry creatures, with plenty of good sense, not only ready to work, but absolutely hating idleness. Mary, who was older than Paul, took somewhat after her father, a tall, handsome girl, though she did not think about the matter; nor did any one else, because they loved her for her good qualities. Janet and Lizzie were very like their mother; and Effie was a fair-haired, blue-eyed

little damsel, not yet five years old, though she, like her
sisters, could assume a sedate air, and help in household
matters in all sorts of ways, besides looking after the pet
animals. Rob, who came next to Janet, was a sturdy
little chap, courageous as a young lion. No pain could
make him cry out, and he could already ride after the
cattle with as much boldness as his elder brothers.
Tommy, the youngest, it must be acknowledged, was
inclined to be a pickle. Effie patronized him, and did
her best to keep him out of mischief, and he, in most
instances, followed her precepts ; though, as yet, he had
done very little towards making himself useful, nor had
he made any great strides in book-learning.

The captain and Mrs. Berrington had felt the difficulty
of educating their children, and had resolved to send the
elder boys and girls to a school at Sydney or Melbourne,
when the captain, while on a journey, happened to stop
at a shepherd's hut towards night to obtain shelter from a
storm which was coming on. The hut-keeper was a
rough-looking fellow, and the captain fully expected to
find the shepherd the same description of person. The
sheep having been folded, the shepherd entered the hut.
What, then, was Captain Berrington's surprise to find
himself addressed in a tone and manner which showed
that the speaker was a gentleman and a person of educa-
tion, as he proved by his conversation, while the small
but well-chosen library on a shelf above his bunk, and a
copy of Horace which he took from his pocket, showed
that the rough life he led did not prevent him from still
indulging in the pleasures of literature.

He had gone through his course at the university, and
had intended entering one of the learned professions,
when he was obliged to visit Australia for his health.
During his absence from home, he heard that every penny
of the property he possessed was lost ; and unable, after

frequent attempts, to obtain employment in the cities, he had, as a last resource, been induced to go into the bush and turn shepherd, hoping ultimately, by the knowledge he would gain, to be able to take some superior situation on an estate. He, however, confessed that he was heartily weary of the life which, it was evident, was rendered doubly disagreeable by the character of his mate, although he uttered no complaint against the man. The term of service for which he had engaged was just about to expire, and Captain Berrington, much pleased with him, invited him, as soon as he should be at liberty, to come to Stratton. In the meantime he made all the inquiries in his power about Mr. Hayward, and was satisfied of the truth of the account he gave of himself. Mr. Martin Hayward was not only a scholar and a gentleman, but was a fair artist, and possessed considerable musical talent; he was, moreover, a true and enlightened Christian. He had spent about a month at Stratton, when Captain Berrington made him an offer to act as tutor to his children. This he had eagerly accepted, and had faithfully fulfilled his trust, never showing the slightest inclination to resign it. The boys were very fond of him, and, for the few hours they were every day engaged in their studies, they worked most diligently. He also afforded Mrs. Berrington considerable help in instructing the girls, so that they were fully as well educated, at all events, as the generality of young ladies.

Mrs. Hugh Berrington received a letter from her husband, saying that his brother Frank and family had arrived, including a Miss Emily Saville, the younger sister of Mrs. Berrington, and that they proposed setting out directly the ladies should have recovered the effects of the sea-voyage. The letter had been some days coming; no time was to be lost, the party might quickly follow. Mrs. Hugh and the girls were busy from morning to night making preparations for the reception of their relatives. Mr. Hayward insisted on putting up a hut for himself near that of the overseer, in order that his room might be devoted to their use; and Paul, answering for Harry, agreed to follow his example. Even then it would require pretty close packing to accommodate the two families.

All preparations had been made, and Mrs. Hugh Berrington began to wish that her relatives would arrive and terminate the period of suspense.

It was nearly two months since the drays had started, when one evening, just as Paul had returned from stocking the cattle, and was on his way home, with his saddle on his arm, he caught sight of a person on horseback galloping towards him.

"It must be Harry!" he cried. "No—yes—it is him! He'll bring us news."

Harry soon came up, and as he threw himself from his steed and shook hands with his brother, exclaimed, "They'll be here soon after dark, and father sent me on that mother might have supper ready, and be prepared for them."

"What sort of people are they? How do you like them?" asked Paul.

"As to that, if we take them in the lot, the less said about them the better. Uncle Frank's a fine fellow, and father seems very glad to have him; but Aunt Augusta —well, you'll see her when she comes. She wishes herself home again, and so do Evelina and Adela, I suspect. The younger boys are jolly little fellows; but Hector— we shall have to break him in—he's just what we thought he'd be. Reginald is more likely to take soon to our ways; he's a manly sort of fellow, and there's some fun in him However, you will soon be able to judge for

yourself about them all; only there's one thing—we must
not let Mr. Hector lord it over us. If he attempts it, we
must take the shine out of him."

Before Harry had told Paul half of what he wanted to
know they reached home, when, as may be supposed,
the whole household was aroused into a state of the
greatest activity.

At last the beds were made, the supper-table was laid,
the lamps were lighted, and all was ready. Mrs. Berrington and her daughters had sat down, and taken up
their work. Two of them had attempted to read, but
found that impossible just then. Biddy was watching
over the pots and pans in the kitchen. The boys were at
the front door, now and then running along the road to
listen, when the cracking of whips, the tramp of horses,
and the sound of wheels was heard.

"Here they come! here they come!" cried the boys,
in chorus.

Paul and Harry lighted their lanterns. "That's Uncle
Frank," exclaimed the latter, as a tall, gentlemanly-look-
ing man rode up alongside their father.

Mrs. Hugh Berrington came out to receive them.
Greetings were over by the time the first dray drew up
at the door. The captain and Mrs. Berrington assisted a
lady to descend, and carried her in their arms into the
house. Two young ladies were next helped out, who
appeared to take very little notice of any one, until Mary
and Janet, hurrying forward, kissed them affectionately,
and welcomed them to Stratton, when they led them into
the sitting-room.

"That's Aunt Augusta, and those two Evelina and
Adela," whispered Harry. "And here comes Sybil, the
youngest; a jolly little bird, isn't she? Then Gertrude,
Edgar, and Albert are with their Aunt Emily in the other
dray. I shouldn't be surprised if Mr. Hector were there

THE FIRST ARRIVAL.

too, for I don't see him on horseback; but here comes
Reginald—he'll want to be introduced, or he'll not speak
to you," and Harry laughed. "Here, Reginald, old
fellow, this is my brother Paul, and these are Rob
and Tommy," exclaimed Harry, as a fine-looking lad rode
up and, dismounting, shook hands with his cousins.

The second dray now drove up, and Hector, a delicate-
looking youth, was the first to get out, stretching himself
and yawning as he did so.

A very nice-looking young lady, whom the children
called "Aunt Emily," followed; and then Gertrude,
Edgar, and Albert, of whom little could be known, as
they did not utter a word, were lifted out.

"Here, lend a hand and help us, you fellows!" said
Paul to his cousins, as he and Harry went to assist their
father and Mr. Berrington, who, with their tutor and
Sandy, were engaged in unloading the drays.

Reginald at once came forward, but Hector, without
replying, sauntered into the house.

The articles as they were taken out were piled up
round the walls of the rooms, leaving but little space
to move about. Mr. Hayward at once went back to his
hut, telling Paul and Harry that he was ready for them,
and that there would be a bed for one of his cousins if he
wished to come up. It was some time after the ladies
had been shown their rooms, before they made their
appearance at the supper-table—Mrs. Berrington leaning
on her husband's arm, the elder girls following, having
changed their travelling dresses for evening costume,
such as was not often seen in the bush. Their cousins,
who wore their usual plain dress, looked at them with no
slight astonishment. Hector came in shortly afterwards,
and took his seat without speaking.

"I am afraid that you must be very tired," remarked
Mrs. Hugh to her sister-in-law.

"Yes, indeed; I wonder that I have survived it coming over those dreadful mountains—sufficient to shake the nerves of the strongest, and mine are sensitive to a degree," was the answer.

"A few days of quiet will set you all to-rights," observed the captain. "Your girls do not appear to be the worse for it, though Hector looks somewhat knocked up."

"Ah, yes! he takes after me," said Mrs. Berrington.

"I'm rather more bored than tired," observed Hector. "I didn't imagine that such a country as this was to be found in the Queen's dominions."

"It's the finest country in the world, old fellow," said Harry, from the other end of the table. "You'll learn to like it in time. So cheer up, we'll soon make a man of you."

Hector turned a disdainful glance towards the speaker.

"Harry, do not let your tongue run loose," observed his father, though with no very angry glance.

The conversation soon became general, Miss Emily Saville doing her best to make amends for her sister's silence. She and her nieces expressed themselves delighted with the delicious fruits offered them, and the evening passed by more pleasantly than might have been expected. Reginald accepted his cousins' invitation to accompany them to their quarters, thus enabling Hector to share his room with Rob and Edgar. It is not necessary to particularize how the rest of the family were stowed away.

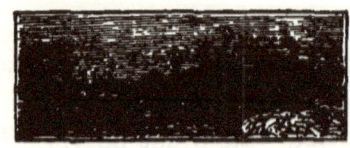

CHAPTER III.

Early Rising—Milking Cows—How to "Bail-up" a Cow—Vicious Animals—Hector Charged, and takes to Flight—Reginald and his Pail upset by a Calf—Tries again, and Succeeds.

"ROUSE up, you fellow, and come and learn how to milk cows!" exclaimed Harry, as, the second morning after the arrival of the party, he, just at the break of day, rushed into his cousin Hector's room. Hector had done nothing the previous day but sit, rod in hand, on the bank of the river, attempting to catch some fish. He now yawned and stretched himself.

"It cannot be time to get up yet—it is scarcely daylight."

"There's light enough to milk the cows, and the cool of the morning is the best time," answered Harry. "Your Aunt Emily and the rest of the girls are there already."

"I'll get up presently, when I've had a little more sleep," said Hector, yawning again.

"No, no; you've got to learn how to do it, and if you don't begin now, you never will. You must learn how to do everything, or you cannot become a prosperous settler. I'll not leave you until I see you up."

Hector reluctantly, and in no good humour, began to dress. As he intended finishing his toilet after his return, he was soon ready.

"Come along! Sandy, Paul, and Reginald are driving in the cows; though we have a few which won't come up to 'the bail,' as they will soon be taught to do; and it will be some fun to you to see how we manage things."

"You don't expect me to milk cows?" said Hector, as they walked along.

"Indeed I do, if you are to have milk for breakfast; it is what young hands like you and the girls are most suited for."

"I am older than you are," exclaimed Hector, looking indignantly at Harry.

"Older in years, but younger in this country. Why, my little brother Rob is of more use than you'll be for months to come, if you don't look sharp about it."

"It's a horrid country, to say the best of it; I wish I hadn't come out here," exclaimed Hector.

"It is my country," answered Harry, "and I'll not have it abused. It is as fine a country as any in the world, or finer, I believe."

"You call that rocky range, which took us three days to get over, a fine country!"

"Ah! that's nothing! you must take the rough with the smooth. I dare say there are quite as many rugged places in England."

"From what I have seen of it, all I can say is, I intend to leave your beautiful country as soon as papa gets back

some of his property. I hope to obtain a commission in
the Guards."

" You'd better try and get a commission in our Black-
guards," answered Harry, laughing. " They are a very
useful body of men, and most of their officers are
gallant fellows."

" Bosh ! " cried Hector, who felt too indignant to make
any other reply.

He, nevertheless, accompanied Harry to the stock-
yard, where they found Mary and Janet with their milk-
pails, and their two elder cousins and Miss Saville.
Within the yard into which the cattle were being driven,
on one side, were two strong posts, about five feet high,
with a cross-piece on the top and another at the bottom,
with a strong rail between them, which could be moved
from side to side and fixed by means of a peg. Just
behind this, but outside the yard, was a windlass, with a
rope passing between the two posts.

" Do you see those posts ? " asked Harry ; " that's
where we milk our cows."

As he spoke he patted a cow on the back, and crying,
" Bail up ! " she walked quickly up and put her head
between the posts, where it was so secured by the rail
that she could not withdraw it. Taking one of the pails,
and seating himself on a stool close by, he commenced
the operation, which, to Hector's intense astonishment,
he performed in a thoroughly efficient manner. Other
cows walked up without the slightest trouble, and were
milked in the same way by his sisters.

" Now, girls, you had better clear out of the yard ! "
shouted Paul ; " we have two or three somewhat restive
animals to deal with."

Mary and Janet, whose pails were by this time full,
followed their brother's advice, and, accompanied by Miss
Saville and their cousins, made their way out of the

yard; while Mr. Hayward, who summoned Harry and
Reginald to his assistance, stood ready at the windlass.
Paul took hold of the rope, which was unwound, with
a noose at the end of it fixed to a long stick, and
approached one of the cows just before driven into the
yard. Immediately he attempted to throw the noose
over her head she swerved, now on one side, now on the
other, taking care never to put her nose to the ground.
At last, however, Paul succeeded in throwing the noose
over her horns, when he drew it tight by a jerk.

"Haul away!" he shouted; and round went the
windlass, the cow, in the meantime, making every effort
to free herself, leaping and bounding, throwing up her
head and trying to shake off the rope. But all was in
vain. Sandy sounded his stock whip at her flanks, now
and then giving her a touch to remind her that it was at
hand, until gradually she was drawn up to the posts and
her head securely fixed, when Sandy approached with the
milk-pail.

"I'm not going to trust you yet, my lady," he said,
fastening her hind legs up on the side on which he was
about to take his seat. This done, he began the operation of milking. He had almost drawn as much as he
expected to obtain, when the cunning cow, finding that
she could not kick over the pail, came down on her side;
and Sandy, with difficulty, made his escape from under
her with the loss of the contents of his pail.

There were two other cows to be milked, which had
been standing by watching attentively the treatment
received by their companion. Paul, taking the rope,
approached one of them. The creature seemed to have
made up her mind not to be milked, and as he drew near
she whisked round with wonderful rapidity, now and
then making as if she would run at him; but Paul was
far too active to be caught. Suddenly her eyes fell on

Hector, who had been ashamed to leave the yard, although greatly longing to do so. Putting down her head, with a loud bellow she rushed towards him.

"Run for it! Spring on one side, and then make a bolt for the palings. I'll help you over!" shouted Harry.

Hector, however, was too much frightened to follow the advice. Instead of facing the cow and watching what she was about to do, he turned round and ran across the slippery yard; before he got far, as might have been expected, down he fell. The next instant the cow would have been upon him, had not Paul, who had been following with the noose, succeeded dexterously in slipping it over her horns, when the windlass being turned rapidly round, she found herself brought up by a violent jerk. In vain she endeavoured to get free. The hide rope which had caught her was strong enough, as Sandy affirmed, "to hold a seventy-four," and she was quickly, in spite of her bellowings and kickings, hauled up to "the bail;" while Hector, much frightened and excessively angry at his accident, picked himself up, and ran to the paling towards which Harry was beckoning him.

Sandy took care on this occasion not to be caught by the cow, and managed to take all the milk he required. Several others were brought up in the same fashion. Two who had been looking on, seeing that, whatever they might do, they would have to submit at last, walked up quietly and poked their heads into "the bail."

"I should like to try and milk a cow," exclaimed Reginald, who felt ambitious to imitate his cousins' example and make himself useful.

"We have two more heifers to milk, and you shall try; but I don't think you will succeed at first," said Paul.

Reginald was determined to make an attempt. As the heifer showed no great inclination to submit to the process—being accompanied by her calf—she was caught by the horns, quickly dragged up to "the bail," and leg-roped. Here she stood quietly enough while Paul stroked her, patted her back, and scratched her about the ears.

"Now, Reginald!" cried Paul, "get your stool and milk-pail, and try what you can do." Neither Paul nor his cousin had observed that the calf—only a few weeks old—which had remained on the other side of the yard, had been stamping and pawing the ground, and exhibiting other signs of indignation at seeing its mother made captive.

Reginald, with sleeves tucked up and eager face, commenced trying to milk, but not a drop could he produce. Suddenly, uttering a loud cry, the calf, with head lowered, made a dash across the yard, sending Reginald flying in one direction, his milk-pail and stool in others, to the great amusement of the lookers-on. Reginald picked himself up, not being really hurt; and although he at first looked very frightened, he soon recovered his equanimity.

"Now, Reginald," said Paul, "you will very likely succeed better this time. Try again."

Reginald had plenty of spirit, and getting the pail and stool, once more sat himself down; and Paul showing him how to work, he managed to draw milk from the heifer.

"Capital!" cried Paul; "but you had better let me finish—one cannot tell how long she may stay quiet."

At breakfast Hector and Reginald gave very different versions of the milking business of the morning. Hector described it as "a nasty, disgusting affair;" while Reginald declared "that it was very good fun, and that he was proud of his own performance, in spite of his misadventure."

CHAPTER IV.

AS much of the time of the young Berringtons was likely to be taken up by their newly-arrived cousins, it was arranged that they and Mr. Hayward should make holiday. As soon, therefore, as Mary and Janet had finished their household duties they invited their cousins to take a walk round the gardens, which they had not yet seen, and along the bank of the river.

" We can show you some pretty views," said Mary.

" You shall see all our pets," added Janet.

" Pray take your sunshades, girls," murmured Mrs. Berrington, who had just come out of her room. " Without them you will spoil your complexions to a certainty, and perhaps suffer from a *coup-de-soleil.* You do not let your daughters go out without them ?" she added, turning to her sister-in-law.

" We never think of such a thing," answered Mrs. Hugh ; " our hats are lined with pith, and broad-brimmed, and we do not mind a few freckles."

The young ladies, acting on their mother's suggestion, took their sunshades, which, it must be confessed, were not altogether useless, although their cousins did very well without them.

They had got a short distance from the house, when Evelina uttered a scream and pointed to a large animal with a long tail, pointed nose, and short arms, which came hopping along at a great rate towards them.

"Oh! what's that monster?" she exclaimed. "How can we get out of its way?"

"That's only our tame kangaroo, Jumper," answered Janet, laughing. "He is a great pet; he has been out with Sandy all the morning, and is now coming to pay his respects to us."

The kangaroo, which was upwards of five feet high, came bounding along, moving himself by the wonderful muscular power of his long hind-legs, though he had in addition to carry his tail, which he lifted off the ground when moving; this tail, however, assisted him to rest when he reached his young mistresses and waited to receive the piece of bread they had brought to give him. Close behind came an animal on four legs.

"Oh! here comes another horrid creature," cried Adela. "A wolf! a wolf!"

"No; we have no wolves here. That is our kangaroo dog Bruce. He and Jumper are great friends, though he would run down and kill any of Jumper's relatives without the slightest remorse. Here, Bruce, Bruce."

A magnificent dog, a mixture of a St. Bernard and greyhound, came up and licked Mary's and Janet's hand, and attempted to treat their cousins in the same way. The young ladies not liking his looks started back, and it was some time before they could be persuaded to pat him on the head. Although Janet called Jumper and

Bruce to accompany them, the latter only obeyed; the former bounded towards the house.

"The rogue has gone to see what he can get in the kitchen; if he can catch Biddy off her guard, he'll snatch up anything he can find, and be away with it," observed Mary.

The menagerie was in the flower-garden, where several of their pets which could not be allowed to remain at liberty were confined. Among the prettiest was a flying squirrel, a little animal with beautiful fur, its legs united by a membrane which enables it to float from the tree-tops to the ground without injury, then to run up the trunk of another, once more to descend, and thus make its way along. Poor little "Fussy!" its habits were nocturnal, and it had been accustomed to roam about at large in the house; but Captain Berrington, fearing that it might disturb his guests, had turned it out of doors to live with several other animals which his children had tamed.

The young ladies had made their way along a path which had been cut through the scrub, close to the banks of the river, that Mary might show her cousins the views she had spoken of. They had been joined by Rob and Edgar, who considered that they could not let them go so far from home without an efficient escort.

"With such valiant guards we may, I think, venture further than we have been accustomed to," said Mary. "We shall have to stoop now and then to get under the vines, or squeeze ourselves between the trunks of the trees. We have no wild animals to fear, and need only be careful not to tread upon a snake."

"A snake!" exclaimed Evelina. "Oh, how dreadful! Let's go home."

"Oh, come on," cried Rob, "I'll clear the road, and kill any snakes which may show their ugly heads."

Flourishing his hatchet, which he drew from his belt, he proceeded to cut away the vines and any branches which impeded their way.

Their progress was of course slow, but Rob asserted that they would soon come out into a more open spot, when they would be able to walk as fast as they liked. The air beneath the shade of the tall trees was deliciously cool compared to the hot atmosphere of the open ground; and even Evelina acknowledged that it was very pleasant. She had not gone far, however, before she shrieked out to Mary—

" You said there were no savage creatures! Look at this monster; it will kill us all!"

" Why, that's only an iguana. It has no teeth, and wouldn't bite you if it had. I'll try and catch it, and you shall have it for dinner; it makes an excellent stew," exclaimed Rob, who heard her cry out.

The iguana, a large species of lizard, was, however, far too quick for Rob, and was away out of sight before he got up to the tree on which he had seen it. Edgar manfully kept up with him, but having no weapon except a clasp knife, he could render but little service in clearing the road. Rob was shouting to the girls to " come on," when suddenly he himself stopped short.

" Edgar, did you see any one?" he asked, in a low voice.

" Yes, a hideous black face; it popped down immediately behind the bushes."

" We had better not go on, then; for though many of the blacks are friendly hereabouts, yet others who come from a distance are very treacherous."

Not stopping to hear more, Edgar scampered away to tell the ladies, who, as soon as they heard the alarming intelligence, began to beat a retreat. They were quickly overtaken by Rob, who had not only seen a black man, but a bundle of spears, and was fully satisfied of the danger of remaining longer in the scrub.

Mary was the first to recover herself. "After all, the boys may have mistaken the stump of a tree for a native; or if they did see a black, he may have come with no bad intentions," she observed; "we need not give up our walk in consequence."

However, her cousins looked so frightened that she led them directly out of the scrub towards the kitchen-garden, intending to go round under a trellis work, which had a thick hedge on the outside, and at that hour of the day afforded a pleasant shady walk. They were passing along that part which was nearest the open ground when they heard the tramp of a horse's hoofs galloping at full speed, and directly afterwards Paul shouting out to Harry—

"Where's our father?"

"He has gone off with Uncle Frank to Gibson's station," answered Harry. "But what's in the wind?"

"The blacks have shown their ugly faces again, not far off. I caught sight of a mob of them just before I passed Jenkins's hut, and when stopping to leave a message I could nowhere find him. The blacks have evidently been there, and, I am afraid, have killed him. I did not stop to search longer, but came on to tell father, that he might send over to Ogilvie to set the police after them."

"I'll ride Bolter, and get Reginald to come with me," answered Harry.

"Reginald! He's no use; he will never keep up with you, and the chances are that he is pitched off before you have galloped a mile. Get Mr. Hayward or Sandy to go with you," said Paul.

"They are both away just now," answered Harry; "but why can't you get a fresh horse and go yourself?"

"Look here," the girls heard Paul say; "one of the black fellows dashed a spear, and gave me this ugly scratch on the side, and I should be foolish to attempt riding so far. I must go in and get mother to doctor it."

The young ladies on hearing this were naturally much alarmed. Mary was about to call to her brothers, but they were already beyond hearing; so she, followed by the rest of the party, hastened to the house that she might break the intelligence to her mother.

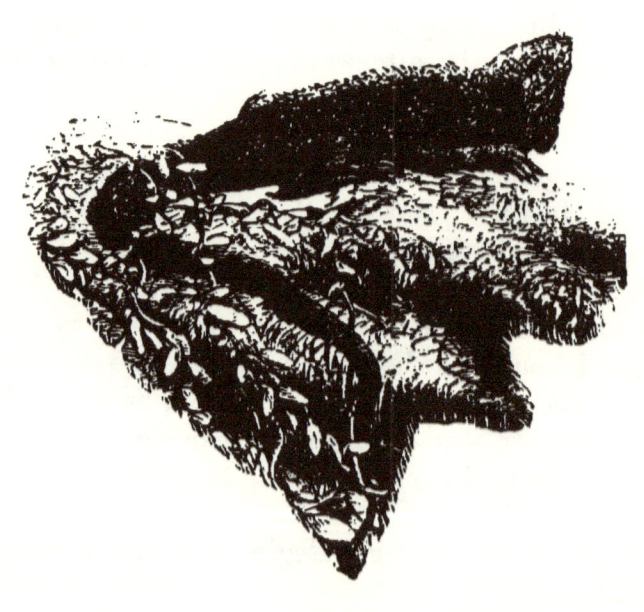

CHAPTER V.

Paul comes Home Wounded—Prepare for an Expected Attack—Hector Missing—The Boys go in Search of Him—Biddy gives the Alarm—Rob and Egdar agree to Keep Watch—The Way they do so—Arrival of the Black Police and their Officer.

AS soon as Mary arrived at home she told her mother what she had heard; and lint, salve, and bandages were speedily got ready.

Paul's pale check when he arrived showed that he was suffering considerably, though he made light of the wound.

" Oh ! it's nothing ! " he said, trying to laugh. " A black fellow's spear merely grazed my side, though had not Polly swerved at that moment it would have stuck into her neck."

" It is a mercy, my boy, that it did not strike you in the back," said Mrs. Hugh Berrington, examining the wound, which she thought far more severe than Paul was inclined to suppose it.

" I had been looking after some cattle which had

D

strayed from one of the herdsmen, a new hand," he said, " when I suddenly found myself close to a mob of strange blacks, the very same, I suspect, Harry and I met with when hunting up Old Bolter. Knowing the imprudence of trusting myself among them, I immediately turned my horse's head and galloped off, but not until several spears had been hurled at me. I felt one pop through my clothes, but I thought that it had given me only a slight scratch. On reaching Jenkins's station, wishing to warn him of the vicinity of the black fellows, I looked about everywhere, but could not find him, and therefore came on that information might be sent to the police without delay, in order that they might proceed in search of the strangers and drive them away. Before returning home I found Mr. Hayward, who, with Harry, has gone over to Ogilvie to give information of the blacks being in the neighbourhood."

" But what if they should come here while our husbands are away ? " exclaimed Mrs. Berrington, trembling with alarm.

" I am here, and this slight hurt won't prevent me from defending you," exclaimed Paul, feeling not a little indignant at his aunt's remark, "and there are Reginald, and Hector, and Sandy, and the other men will be back before long."

"And *we* can fight too," exclaimed Janet. " I know how to fire a pistol, so does Mary."

" What a fearful state of things ! " ejaculated Mrs. Berrington

"Oh, aunt, you'll soon get accustomed to it," said Janet, who often spoke very like Harry.

" I hope that we shall not be reduced to such extremities," said Aunt Emily. " But where are Reginald and Hector ? "

" I saw Reginald at our hut ; I told him to come on here

in case he might be wanted, but as to Hector, I do not know where he is."

" Suppose he should be fishing by the river, and the blacks should find him. They may kill the poor boy," exclaimed Mrs. Berrington.

Though Paul thought this more than possible, should Hector have gone to any distance, he tried to reassure his aunt, intending to go himself and try and find his cousin.

When, however, he attempted to move, he discovered that he could not do so without great pain and difficulty. He was thankful when Reginald came in, and Rob at the same time making his appearance, he sent the two off in search of Hector, warning them to keep away from any place which might conceal a lurking enemy. He then held a consultation with Mary and Janet, and arranged with them how they might best prepare the house for defence, should the blacks attack it. They all knew that there was not much real danger provided that they were not taken by surprise, as the natives, unaccustomed to the use of fire-arms, were sure to run away if sturdily withstood. He knew he could depend upon his two elder sisters, though he suspected that his cousins would not prove heroines.

The day wore on, the captain and his brother were not expected until late. Reginald and Rob had not returned from their search for Hector, and Sandy, whom they expected, had not yet made his appearance.

The sun set, and darkness came on ; the girls agreed to watch in different directions, from whence they could command the approaches to the house. Biddy was naturally stationed at the kitchen end of the house, which looked towards the bush. Poor Mrs. Berrington's alarm became greater and greater.

Mrs. Hugh and her daughters were doing their best to

keep her from fainting by the due application of sal
volatile, though they themselves could scarcely restrain
their own fears.

Suddenly a fearful shriek ran through the house; it
came from Biddy. Mary and Janet hurried round,
shutting the doors opening on the verandah where they
had been stationed, and rushed towards her.

" Sure, the nagers are coming! the nagers are
coming!" they heard her again and again shriek out.
She was, however, at her post at the door, but had
thrown her apron over her head. Before closing the
door, the courageous girls looked out to ascertain how
far off the natives were from the house. There, sure
enough, they saw three figures approaching with what
looked like long spears in their hands.

" Arrah! come in, me darlin's, and don't let the nagers
catch ye!" shrieked Biddy.

" What's all that hullabaloo about?" exclaimed one of
the figures, approaching, and Hector, and Reginald, and
Rob came up to the door.

Biddy, however, who had stopped her ears as well as
hid her face, still fancied that they were blacks, and continued shrieking as loudly as ever.

" Run, Rob, and tell mother and aunt that you have
come back safe, while we try and bring this foolish girl
to her senses," said Mary.

It was, however, some minutes before Biddy could be
quieted, and assured by the sight of the young masters
that it was they whom she had seen, and that no natives
had shown themselves.

Reginald then told Mary that they had found Hector
fast asleep on the bank, while his fishing-rod was floating
in the middle of a water-hole, and that they had spent
some time in attempting to recover it. Though the boys
had returned safe, and one cause of anxiety was removed,

there was still a possibility that the blacks would attack the place, should they have been on the watch, and have discovered that the gentlemen were away.

Paul, however, did not think this likely, as, had they been lurking about, they would certainly have caught the boys, and perhaps have killed them. Poor Mrs. Berrington continued bemoaning her hard fate in coming to such a country.

"But, my dear Augusta," said Mrs. Hugh, "no harm has happened to those we love, and we ought not to mistrust God. You and I have gone through numerous trials and troubles, and have been mercifully preserved through them all."

At length the captain and his brother returned, and, having heard nothing of the blacks, were greatly surprised at the state of agitation into which the family had been thrown. The captain commended Paul for his judgment in sending for the police. Taking their firearms with them, they at once went back to let Sandy and the other men know that the blacks had been seen near the house, that they might be on their guard.

"They are not likely to be surprised while Bruce is on the watch," observed Paul; "he can scent a black a hundred yards off."

Poor Mrs. Berrington was thus again made anxious, fearing that her husband and the captain might be attacked before they got back to the house. At last they made their appearance, reporting that Sandy and the men were on the watch at the stock-yards, but that Harry and Mr. Hayward had not yet returned; indeed, the captain believed that they would probably accompany the police, or, at all events, not come back until the morning.

The children were put to bed, and the ladies were at length persuaded to retire to rest. The captain and Mr.

Berrington arranged to keep watch and watch, so that they might run no risk of being surprised. Paul wanted to join them, but his father insisted that he should remain quiet, lest his wound, trifling though he considered it, might become inflamed. Hector went into his room without offering his services. Mr. Berrington looked vexed, but said nothing; possibly he thought that he would go to sleep at his post, and thus be worse than useless.

"I say, Edgar, though we are sent to bed, we are not bound to go to sleep," exclaimed Rob. "I vote that you and I keep watch at the window, turn and turn about. I have got one of Paul's pistols, and if any blacks come we will shoot them."

"But they would have to come fearfully close to do that, and I don't think I could fire at a man with a spear in his hand, grinning horribly at me out of the dark."

It is easy to imagine the picture Edgar conjured up.

"That's the very time I would shoot," answered Rob; "if I did not, he might hurl the spear and stick it into me."

"Keep quiet, you fellows," growled out Hector, who was awakened by their talking, though he did not hear what they said. They were silent till they thought that he was again asleep.

"If you're afraid I'm not," said Rob. "I will take the first watch, and I will call you when it's time for you to look out, and then you can rouse me up if you see anything, and I will be alongside you in a moment."

Edgar having agreed to this, Rob sat himself down on a stool, with his head just above the window-sill, on which it soon dropped. He was, in reality, fast asleep, though all the time he thought that he was keeping a very bright look-out, and that he saw savages creeping up in the distance, but that he was waiting to give the alarm until they should get somewhat closer. At last he awoke with a most uncomfortable crick in his neck, and found, to his surprise, that the dawn had broken. Hector and Edgar were sleeping soundly, and believing that no blacks would venture near the house by daylight, he wisely crept into his bunk, where he lay until roused by the sound of the gong which summoned the family to prepare for breakfast.

The night had passed without any appearance of the blacks, and the captain, who had searched round the house in every direction, could find no traces of them. He began, indeed, to suspect that Rob must have been mistaken in supposing that he had seen a lurking native in the scrub. He and Mr. Berrington, followed by Bruce, after breakfast made a long circuit through the scrub, and visiting the spot Rob described, the captain had reason to change his opinion, for he at length found traces of natives, and the remains of a fire, where they must have encamped that very night. This satisfied him that the precautions he had taken had not been useless, but, as far as he could judge, the blacks had retreated to the westward. The chief anxiety of the family was now about Harry and Mr. Hayward, who had not yet returned. Late in the day, however, Rob and Edgar, who were patrolling round and round the house under the idea that they were keeping guard, saw Harry galloping up to them.

" Well, what news ? " shouted Rob. " We have been expecting the blacks all day, but they have not come yet· Have you fallen in with them ? "

" Yes, indeed we have ! " answered Harry, " and had a desperate fight too. We killed some of them, and the rest ran off. Lieutenant Bertram, of the police, believes that they will still remain lurking in the neighbourhood, and has come on with some of his men to be ready to act

as a guard to the house should father wish it. We have
had some exciting work, let me tell you. It was wonderful
the way our black police hunted down their countrymen;
but I must not stop, as they will be wanting to know at
home what has happened."

Dismounting, Harry hurried into the house, while his
younger brother led his tired steed to the paddock.

ARRIVAL OF THE BLACK POLICE.

Harry had just made his report, and Mrs. Hugh was
busy in preparing some food for their expected visitors,
when Mr. Hayward, accompanied by a young officer, rode
up to the door, closely followed by a dozen black troopers,
in dark blue and red uniforms. Mr. Hayward introduced
Lieutenant Bertram, who explained his reasons for
coming.

Mrs. Berrington was profuse in her thanks. "We have

THE TROOPERS AT SUPPER.

had a dreadful fright, Mr. Bertram, and I hope that you and your men will remain here until the blacks are driven out of the country. I shall get no rest, night or day."

" I am afraid, madam, that will not be so easy an operation as you suppose," answered the lieutenant. "The blacks have an idea that they are the owners of the soil, and that we are intruders, and they are not very willing to decamp. Our business is rather to keep them in order, and prevent them from attacking the whites."

As Harry explained that they had been a good many hours without eating, supper was immediately placed on the table, while provisions were carried out to the troopers, who sat down in a circle on the grass-plot—it could not be dignified as a lawn—with their horses picketed near them. The ladies went out to see them as they sat in the sunlight, not at all inconvenienced by its glare. They seemed merry, careless fellows, laughing and chattering away in their own curious lingo—a mixture of English and native words.

Mr. Bertram said they were all blacks from a distance, composed of two or three different tribes who could not understand each other's original language. The captain was grieved to find that there was little doubt that his shepherd had been murdered, although his body had not been discovered. The flock had been driven to a station nearer home, where two of the police had been left to watch the hostile natives, although it was not at all likely that they would for the present make another attack.

Poor Mrs. Berrington saw, with much regret, the lieutenant and his men take their departure. They were going, he said, to make another thorough search for the hostile natives, and to advise them to remove to a distance from the white men's stations.

CHAPTER VI

Pleasant Rides through the Country—Magnificent Vegetation—Hector Stung by a Nettle—A Hurricane—Roof of the Hut Blown off.

SOME weeks passed away, and the new comers were getting accustomed to bush life. Even the unimpressible Evelina and Adela began to take an interest in what was going on, though they were still open to the criticism pronounced on them by Harry to Reginald—

"Those girls of yours are very well in their way, but it is a pity they cannot learn to make themselves useful."

Aunt Emily was, however, delighted with all she saw —the trees, the birds, the animals; and much indeed there was to admire during the rides she and two or three of the girls were accustomed to take, either with Mr. Berrington or Paul, Harry or Reginald.

All apprehension of an attack from the blacks had subsided, and they frequently rode to a considerable distance from Stratton. The country beyond the scrub was open, or rather only sprinkled with tall ungainly gum-trees, but there was to be found in many spots other and very beautiful foliage. In some places groves of acacia trees with yellow blossoms, and in other spots tall coral trees with long pendulous red flowers, looking exactly like strings of coral hanging from the dark foliage. Sometimes they came upon the curiously-shaped bottle tree, which greatly resembles a lemonade bottle placed in the ground. Then, not far off, would be found the grass tree, from the summit of which long pendants projected like enormous blades of grass. Even these trees were of considerable height. Mr. Berrington said that during the hot months he always had a supply of the wood, as the smoke arising from it emits not only a very pleasant odour, but is much objected to by the mosquitos, and by burning it in the room those pests of Queensland are always driven out.

One of the most remarkable trees they met with was the bunya-bunya, a species of pine. It towered like a pinnacle above all the other trees, reaching a height of upwards of two hundred feet.

Some of the young trees were peculiarly handsome, throwing out branches all around close to the ground to a distance of many yards, and smaller branches rising in regular gradation to the top, thus forming a perfect cone with so dense a foliage that it was evident no animal could penetrate it. At the top of the older trees grew an enormous cone of fruit, each being the size of a chestnut. From some of these a bare pole shot up nearly a hundred feet above the branches, with this prodigious cone at the summit. Notwithstanding this, the party saw a couple of blacks belonging to a friendly tribe, who occasionally camped near them, climb to the top, whence they threw down the fruit in handfuls. Harry and Reginald filled their pockets with some of it, which they carried home.

It was cooked as chestnuts are, but was pronounced more farinaceous and much nicer to eat.

THE BOTTLE TREE—(*See* p. 45.)

The party frequently took provisions with them, and enjoyed a picnic in some beautiful spot while their horses were hobbled near. On one of these occasions Hector had condescended to accompany them. He and Paul, with Mr. Hayward, were walking some little distance from the rest, when Hector, not taking an interest in the conversation of his cousin and the dominie, sauntered away from them. Hector had the habit as he walked along of pulling off the leaves of any shrub or tree he passed, from mere thoughtlessness, not with any idea of examining their shape or character.

"Where's Hector got to?" suddenly exclaimed Paul.

"There he is," said Mr. Hayward; then he shouted, "Come back, Hector; come back! Don't touch those shrubs."

But Hector either did not hear or did not heed the call, and Mr. Hayward and Paul set off to run after him. Presently they heard him shriek out, and throw down a large leaf like that of a mallow, which he had plucked from a shrub about fifteen feet in height.

"That's a nettle tree," exclaimed Mr. Hayward; "poor fellow! he'll suffer for it."

They found Hector wringing his hand, and declaring that he had been stung by a snake. He was somewhat consoled when Mr. Hayward and Paul assured him that he had only by mistake caught hold of a huge nettle, though he might expect to suffer from its effects for some days to come. He wanted to run off to a stream near which the party had picnicked, to cool his hand in the water.

"That will only make matters worse," said Paul; "you must keep your hand as dry as possible, for every time you wet it the pain will come on again."

Poor Hector could scarcely refrain from crying out with pain.

"You must grin and bear it, old fellow," said Harry, really wishing to console him. "When you get home mother will, I dare say, apply some remedy. We were fortunately warned about catching hold of nettles before we had your experience; but you'll never do it again."

All the party enjoyed the ride, except poor Hector, who complained bitterly of the pain he suffered from the stinging-nettle. On their arrival at home, Mrs. Hugh applied ammonia and oil. At length he acknowledged that the pain had considerably abated, but during the remainder of the evening he took every opportunity of abusing the country and "its horrible productions."

Harry, who was always ready to take up the cudgels in favour of his native land, answered, "Why, even you in England have got nettles, and poisonous berries too, and, I am sure, have not got one-tenth part of the fruits and plants which this country can produce. We can grow the sugar-cane, cotton, coffee, rice and tobacco, and Peruvian bark, or what answers as well, and spices of all sorts, while few of our berries are poisonous; and, except those rascally dingos, we have not an animal in the country which can do any harm to man or beast."

"Oh, yes! it's a very nice land indeed," sneered Hector.

"Come, old fellow, you're shut up, after all," exclaimed Harry, triumphantly, "and it is time to go to bed. I'm off to our hut. Come along, Reggy; Paul went there an hour ago."

Family prayers were over. The two lads, wishing their fathers and mothers and all hands good night, set off to their abode.

Mr. Hayward and the rest of the inmates of the hut had been some time asleep, when they were awakened by a fearful uproar, like the howling, shrieking, and hissing of a thousand locomotive engines dashing on at full speed —so Reggy described it. They could scarcely hear their own voices as they shouted to know what was happening.

"A storm, lads, and such a one as we don't often get," said Mr. Hayward, who was dressing as fast as he could. The rest followed his example, for at any moment the roof of their hut might be carried off. As they looked out they saw the tallest trees bending and groaning under the fearful blast. At that moment a huge branch, broken off, was dashed to the ground near them with a tremendous crash, while the whole air was filled with leaves, twigs, and smaller branches.

The thunder, which had been heard at a distance, came near. At first it sounded like a faint cannonading, but now it broke overhead with terrible roars and rattles, as if a pitched battle were raging amid the clouds, drowning all other sounds. In such rapid succession did peal follow peal, that they appeared like one continuous roar.

Black clouds made the night as dark as pitch, until the lightning burst forth and lit up the whole of the surrounding scene. Streams of the electric fluid, running down the stems of the tall trees, went hissing along the ground like fiery serpents. Blast succeeded blast, until suddenly the whole roof of the hut, being lifted together, was carried off, the inmates knew not where; when down came the rain in a sheet of water, rather than drops. The lads were thankful that they had got on their clothes, at all events, and had time to slip into their waterproofs.

"We must go and see what is happening at the house. I only hope the fencing won't be blown down, or we shall have work enough to-morrow to collect the stock again," cried Paul.

In spite of the storm, and the danger they ran from falling boughs, they commenced making their way towards the house. Sometimes it was so dark that they could not see a foot before them. Then, in an instant, a bright flash would illumine the whole scene, and they rushed forward again, stopping when darkness came upon them. At length they calculated that they must be close to the house. A flash revealed it to them, but it appeared as if the roof had gone. No one was to be seen. They shouted, but no reply came. They tried to open the door, but it was fastened within. Perhaps those they loved had been crushed by the falling roof. The thought was too dreadful. Paul and Harry shook at the door, and shouted again and again.

CHAPTER VII.

PAUL and Harry, who had run on first, kept knocking and knocking at the door, and shouting at the top of their voices, but the creaking of the verandah posts, the rattling of the shingles on the roof, the continuous roar of the thunder, and the howling of the wind among the trees, completely drowned their voices. They ran round to try and find an entrance by one of the windows or back door, but the shutters were all closed. At length Mr. Hayward and Reggy came up, but they were not more successful in making the inmates hear when they knocked and shouted at the front door. Harry proposed climbing up and dropping down through the opening in the roof. A large portion of the verandah had been torn away, but the beams remained.

" You forget, Harry," shouted Paul in his ear, " we may

E 2

reach the roof, but how shall we get down without the risk of breaking our legs over the fragments which may have fallen in, or the tables and chairs? Stay a moment! There's a rope in the harness room, and if that has not been blown away I'll get it."

Paul recollecting where he had last seen the rope, was able to lay his hand on it, even in the dark. He soon groped his way back.

Harry having proposed the expedition, climbed up first, Paul handing him the rope. He soon reached a rafter, and lowering the rope until he knew that it touched the ground, he fastened it securely, and at once descended, followed by Paul. They had dropped into their own bed-room, which they had given up to Hector; after feeling about, however, they decided he was not there. Neither were Rob nor Edgar. They then groped their way along the passage at the back of the house, to the sitting-room end. During a momentary lull of the storm they thought they heard voices. On opening the door, they presented themselves to the astonished eyes of their family.

Mr. Berrington, aided by Mrs. Hugh and Miss Saville, was endeavouring to calm the fears of his wife and elder daughters, who were well nigh in hysterics, while Mary and Janet were attending to the children—who, poor little things, were naturally very much frightened. Hector, who had got his hand wet, was crying out that he had been bitten by a scorpion, forgetting how he had been stung by a nettle the previous morning. The captain, meantime, was doing his best to keep the windows closed, with the assistance of Biddy, who was bringing him such pieces of wood as she could find to nail up against them, for they threatened to give way, when the wind would have blown out the only lamp which was burning on the table in the centre of the room.

"Where have you boys come from?" asked their father; "I thought all the doors were shut."

"So they are," shouted Paul, "but we came down through the roof.'

"What! were you blown all this way?" asked Mr. Berrington, looking up.

"Not exactly," answered Harry, "we came on our legs."

"Has your hut been blown down?" asked their father.

"The best part of it, on a night like this—the top has," answered Harry.

Paul then explained that Mr. Hayward and Reggy were all this time waiting outside, not knowing how to get in. The captain would not let them open the door, however, without his assistance, and they all three accordingly repaired to it.

"Are you still there?" shouted Harry.

A voice answered, "Yes."

"Stand by to close the door again," said the captain, and slightly opening it, in rushed Reggy and Mr. Hayward, when the whole party, pressing hard, once more closed it, though the blast which came in sent several of the articles of furniture rattling down.

"How, in the name of wonder, did you get in?" exclaimed Reggy, when he found Paul and Harry inside.

He could scarcely believe it when they told him how they had managed to find an entrance. The door being secured, they hastened back to the sitting-room. It was no easy matter to carry on a conversation amid the wild uproar, though the captain, accustomed to storms at sea, made himself heard. He could not tell how much of the roof had gone, for, even through a small aperture the rain made its way in torrents. He was thankful that any part remained which could afford them shelter. Paul could give no account of how it fared with Sandy and the men at the stock-yard. Mr. Hayward volunteered to go back and ascertain, but the captain would not allow this. "You ran risk enough in coming, and I am thankful that you have escaped," he said.

Nothing more could now be done until daylight, as the whole house was in darkness, for as soon as the lamp was lighted in any part, except in the sitting-room, it was blown out again by the wind which made its way through the roof. The captain did not express his fears to the rest of the party, with the exception of Mr. Hayward and Paul, but his chief anxiety was about the river. On listening at the side of the house nearest to it, they could hear the water rushing along its hitherto dry bed, evidently at headlong speed. Mr. Hayward, ever ready to assist, offered to go out and ascertain how high it had risen.

"We may remain here in safety at present, I trust," said Captain Berrington: "it is still a dozen feet below us, probably more, and unless it should rise much higher, we should only unnecessarily expose the ladies to this tremendous rain and the fearful danger of falling branches were we to quit the house. We must, however, keep a watch upon it and escape in time."

Several terrific blasts came, which threatened to blow down the house, or tear off the whole roof. The wind, after the last, began to lull, and the rain ceased. The house, with the exception of the sitting-room, was in such a condition that the family were compelled to remain in that apartment. The night wore slowly away, and every one was thankful when daylight at last returned. Sad indeed was the havoc which had been committed by the tempest; but the captain was thankful that none of the family had been injured, and not a word of complaint escaped him.

No time was lost in commencing to repair the damages.

While Biddy was trying to get her kitchen in order and light a fire, Janet and Mary, with pails and mops, assisted by their cousins, were busily employed in "swabbing decks," as their father called it, and hanging up the wet bedding to dry.

The captain and his brother, with Mr. Hayward, got the carpenter's tools, and commenced repairing the roof, while the younger boys collected all the shingles they could find. Paul, Harry, and Reggy started off to the stock-yards, to see how things fared there, and to assist Sandy and the men if necessary. Before going they took a glance at the river. Reggy could scarcely believe that it was the same stream he had seen the day before, as it now went foaming and rushing by, carrying huge trunks of trees and dead cattle in its vortex, while it appeared four times as broad as before.

"We have often had it as high as this in a rainy season, although it has seldom risen so high at other times," said Paul.

Hector declared that his hand hurt him too much to allow him to do anything, although he at length condescended, when summoned by his sisters, to try and put his own room in order.

As the lads went along, they observed the havoc which had been produced by the storm. Several tall trees had been blown down, others denuded of their branches. The maize was beaten to the ground, the kitchen garden had suffered greatly, and flower-blossoms had everywhere been torn off, while many of the fruit-trees were destroyed.

"It cannot be helped," said Paul, "happily, things grow here very rapidly, and in a short time we shall have all to rights again."

Reginald thought Paul a great philosopher, but he only spoke the truth. They met Sandy coming to ask how the family had fared; he reported more favourably of the stock-yard than Paul had expected. A portion of the roof of some of the buildings had been blown off; but the strong fences intended to resist the charge of a fierce bull or angry heifer had withstood the strongest blasts.

"We ken weel where our weak points are," observed Sandy; "we will soon get things to rights."

Every one had enough to do during that and several following days. The buildings were re-roofed, the fallen trees were sawn through and dragged out of the way to be split up or burned. The garden fences were repaired, and everything else put to rights. Meantime the river had fallen almost to its usual level, though the water holes were united, and it now ran in a regular current. The captain's chief regret was for his maize crop; nothing could restore that, and he expected to obtain scarcely a quarter of the produce he had looked for. It would be necessary, therefore, to dispatch the drays some hundreds of miles to obtain flour, and this must be done as soon as possible, before the regular rainy season should set in. It would not last long, but during that time many of the creeks would be impassable, and other places might be flooded.

There was so much to be done that Captain Berrington did not wish to go himself, and though Paul was always very useful at home, he determined to send him in charge of the party. Paul would have liked to take either Harry or Reggy, but they now worked so well together that his father was unwilling to separate them, besides which they were able to do a great deal of work, and had in addition to attend some hours in the day to their studies, as Mr. Hayward had resumed his duties as tutor, the girls, as well as the boys, regularly attending the school.

Paul could not but feel proud at being so thoroughly trusted by his father, and he hoped to perform his commission well; although he would gladly have had a companion in his long and tedious journey.

The men who accompanied him had been some time in the captain's employ, and were considered thoroughly trustworthy. He himself felt much more anxious about the family. It was not only possible that the blacks might return and cause them alarm, but he might not obtain flour where he expected to find it. Although they would not in consequence be actually in want of food, it would be a considerable privation to have to go without bread. The captain had also confided to him a project Mr. Berrington and he had in view, of forming a new station further up the country. They had not, however, fixed on it; but beyond the ranges to the north-west the captain had heard that a fine region existed, and he proposed forming a party to explore it. He had promised Paul that he should go, and told him that he proposed setting off at the termination of the rainy season. Paul, having bid farewell to his family, accompanied by Harry and Reggy, who were going to see him a few miles on the way, rode after the drays, which had started at daybreak that morning.

The two boys returned towards evening, reporting all well. Paul was much missed; even Hector complained that he had not now a companion to talk to. Although Harry and Reggy were merry fellows, it was generally acknowledged that they were not equal to Paul.

" I trust we shall have him back soon," said his mother, after he had been gone some time ; " although I wish that tidings of him had reached us."

CHAPTER VIII.

A Kangaroo Hunt—Chasing Emus—A pack of Dingoes put to Flight.

REGGY had by this time learned to make himself almost as useful as Harry. Their great delight was riding after stray cattle and horses, which afforded them constant occupation. Occasionally they visited the sheep stations, to see that all was right, or to give directions to the shepherds. Sometimes they drove one of the drays carrying provisions and stores, a task which was not so pleasant as galloping over the country. Now and then Hector was persuaded to join them in the former duty, but he would never even attempt to learn to drive a dray.

"If I could manage to get hold of a well-built dog-cart from London, I should have no objection to turn out a tandem," he said, as he contemptuously surveyed the dray.

As the captain was convinced that "all work and no play makes Jack a dull boy," he occasionally allowed all hands who could be spared to go out hunting, the game being kangaroos or emus, when Bruce and the other dogs at the station had an active part to play. Hector, who rode pretty well, had no objection to join in it. Even Rob and Edgar were at times allowed to go out.

The damage caused by the storm having been repaired, about a week after Paul left home a hunting party was organized, the captain and Mr. Haward joining it, with all the boys. Sandy, on such occasions, always remained at home, although he had learned to stick to the saddle as well as any man. Hunting was not to his taste; besides which, he considered it his duty to look after the ladies at the house and the cattle at the station.

It was a lovely morning, not a cloud was in the sky. The air was so pure, and so fine a breeze was blowing, that no one felt the heat. The boys were in high spirits as they rode along on their sturdy little horses, with the dogs barking and frisking around them. They had not gone far before a large kangaroo was sighted—an " old man," as the big kangaroos are called by the settlers. He was employed in plucking the leaves from some shrubs which partly concealed him. So busily engaged was he, that he did not at first notice their approach, but as they got near his quick ear detected the sound of their horses' feet, and taking one glance at them over his shoulder, he bounded off to seek safety in flight.

The dogs gave chase, the horsemen followed close upon their heels. The kangaroo appeared to move but slowly, and to be making his long bounds with deliberation.

" We shall be up to him in three minutes!" cried Reggy.

" Not so fast as that, by a long way," answered Harry; " he is now going at double the speed you suppose, and will soon increase it."

Harry was right. On went the kangaroo towards a

creek in which there were two or three deep water-holes, a couple of miles to the northward. Hector and Reginald could not help laughing as they saw the wonderful bounds he made, holding his little front claws close to him, as a man does when running a race, with his knowing head held upright. Sometimes, when passing through high grass, the head and shoulders alone were visible, and the dogs could not be perceived except by the waving grass, while often they could not see the chase; still they kept on in its tracks. At last a large water-hole was reached, the kangaroo leapt into it, and having gained the centre, turned round and watched for the approach of the dogs. Bruce—knowing old fellow—was well aware that the kangaroo would have him at a great disadvantage, and contented himself by standing at the edge and barking, as he knew the animal must in time abandon his present position and again take to flight. All the older dogs imitated Bruce's example; but two young ones, thinking themselves braver than their companions, swam out, expecting to catch the kangaroo by the neck and bring him down. The first which approached was caught in his short arms before the dog could seize his throat, and was held down under the water, the kangaroo looking round all the time with perfect unconcern. In vain the dog struggled: the greater its efforts to free himself, the more rapidly the water entered its mouth.

The second dog attempted to make a diversion in its favour, but the kangaroo managed to give it a blow with the sharp claw of one of its hinder feet, and, with a yelp of pain, it swam back to the shore, leaving a ruddy stain in the water, while the body of the first dog which had been seized floated up deprived of life.

Harry and Reggy, with Mr. Hayward, who were leading, now came up, but the kangaroo observing one side of the water-hole unguarded, suddenly, with a few bounds, reached it and made off before the dogs could get round to seize him. Away he went, bounding on as before towards the scrub in which he might have hoped to obtain shelter. The horsemen lost some little time in first getting the dead dog out of the water-hole and by crossing the creek; but they soon recovered their lost ground, as the kangaroo was becoming wearied with his exertions.

A thick scrub was ahead, and directly in front were some large trees. The dogs got almost near enough to catch hold of the tail of the kangaroo, when renewing his exertions, he managed to jump up close to one of the big trees, and to turn round with his back to the trunk. Here he stood at bay, showing, however, not the slightest sign of fear. As the dogs came barking fiercely round it, Reggy, wishing to display his courage, leapt off his horse, and was on the point of running up to the kangaroo when Mr. Hayward shouted to him to stop; and he had soon good reason to be thankful that he had done so, for another of the young dogs getting within reach of the kangaroo, it struck out with one of its hind-claws and inflicted a terrible wound on its assailant. The dog, uttering a yelp of pain, endeavoured to crawl away, but before it did so another blow stretched it dead in front of the kangaroo as a warning to its companions.

It seemed cruel, after the animal had so bravely fought for his life, to destroy him; but, as he would probably have killed more of the dogs, Mr. Hayward fired and finished his career.

The kangaroo was quickly skinned, his long tail being secured to one of the saddles. The best part of the meat, being wrapped in large leaves, was hung up in the shade, to be carried home on their way back. The remainder was left as a trap to the dingoes, whom it was hoped would remain feasting, and be shot by the party on their return.

The object of the expedition, however, was to hunt
emus. Leaving the scrub, they reached some open downs
of wide extent. Keeping, by the captain's directions, on
the lee side, they rapidly advanced, with a bright look-
out ahead. The emu will run from human beings, especially from blacks. It is not, however, afraid either of
horses or drays. It greatly resembles, in size and shape,
the ostrich; but its colour is of a uniform brownish-black
with feather-like hairs in lieu of feathers, and it has no
wings, but its legs being very strong it can run at a rapid
rate. As its head reaches seven feet or more from the
ground it can obtain a wide view over the plain.

Mr. Hayward, who well understood the habits of the
bird, rode on in front. At length he made a sign that
he saw emus in the distance, when the whole party, as
had been arranged, dismounted and led on their horses,
keeping them between themselves and the emus. They
were thus able to get within a couple of hundred yards,
when the wingless birds showed signs of alarm. Mr.
Hayward gave the signal to mount, and leaping on his
horse the rest followed his example, and the emus set off
running at a speed calculated to try the mettle of the fleetest
horse and the endurance of the dogs. The pack, with
loud yelps, bounded after them, followed by the horsemen,
whose object was to keep them together.

The emus had no intention of being caught, but they
had the wind against them, which somewhat impeded
their progress. Two, however, showed signs of flagging,
and the dogs got up to them. It would have been better
for them had they kept at a respectful distance, for the
hindmost emu kicking out struck one of them on the
chest, and sent it flying among its companions. The rest
of the pack taking warning kept out of reach of the
bird's powerful feet. At length one of the hard-pressed
creatures dropped to the ground, where it was speedily

CHASING EMUS.

despatched by the captain, while Mr. Hayward and the boys galloped after the remainder of the flock. Two more were run down and killed in the same manner. The skins were soon taken off and thrown across the horses' necks. A portion also of the flesh was secured, as Harry, Reggy, and Edgar expressed a strong wish to taste it.

The party then commenced their return home. On reaching the spot where the kangaroo had been killed, they caught sight of a pack of dingoes, to which they gave chase. Bruce and his companions pulled down several of these pests to the settler, and others were shot. Not a particle of kangaroo remained on the ground. The dingoes had been unable to reach the meat hung up among the branches, although, from the appearance of the trampled ground beneath, they had evidently made great efforts to get at it. There were numbers of flies, however, buzzing around, and in a very few hours it would have been uneatable. This was only one of several kangaroo and emu hunts in which the boys took a part. Even Hector acknowledged that there was some fun in the sport, though he should like to have turned out in a red coat and riding-cap.

"With the thermometer at ninety in the shade?" remarked Harry. "I don't think you would ride out a second time in such a fashion."

CHAPTER IX.

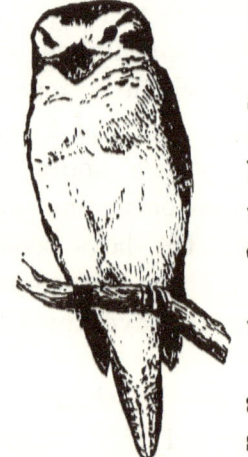

THINGS went on quietly enough at
the farm, until one day Biddy
struck—not for wages, but for help.
She could not bear to see the young
ladies do the work they were compelled
to do, and yet it was more than she
could do herself.

The captain inquired whether she
would object to a black help.

"Sure not, yer honour, if she kapes
a dacent tongue in her mouth," answered Biddy.

So the captain rode out to obtain the assistance Biddy
asked for. A short distance away, a small tribe of
friendly blacks were encamped; among them was one
called Bendigo. He had frequently visited the station,
and was ready to make himself generally useful by
chopping wood or occasionally assisting the shepherds.
He had a wife named Betty, who, if she was not pretty
to European notions, was thought to be so by Bendigo,
and she was a young, good-natured, merry little woman.

The captain invited the couple to come and take up their abode on the farm. They were to have a hut to themselves. Betty was to help Biddy, and Bendigo was to do any work required of him. The offer was accepted, and Betty was forthwith installed as Biddy's help. Her costume when she made her appearance was not altogether suited to her new style of life, as it consisted of a man's old shirt and a piece of grass matting as a petticoat.

The young ladies immediately manufactured for her a robe of blue serge trimmed with red braiding, while Biddy initiated her into the use of soap and water, to which she had hitherto been a stranger. She carefully brushed her hair and combed it out with a horse-comb, none of those in ordinary use being strong enough for the purpose.

Betty was immensely proud of her new costume, and hurried away to exhibit herself to her husband and the other black fellows on the station. Had not Bendigo stopped her she would have gone off to the camp; but he, not without reason, feared that she might have been deprived of her new dress by some of her beloved relatives.

Every morning she appeared at daybreak, and if Biddy overslept herself she was sure to awaken her by loudly knocking at the door of the kitchen in which Biddy slept. They were very good friends, though neither could understand a word the other said. But Betty quickly learned, after a certain sort, Biddy's language, and, as may be supposed, a very curious lingo was the result. Harry declared that any day Betty might be taken for a black Irish girl.

"Sure we have no naguers in the ould country, Master Harry!" answered Biddy.

Betty soon learned to perform any work she was shown how to do; but she preferred tending the children, and if she saw them running down to the river, or wandering too far from the house, she was after them like a shot, always bringing them back in her arms, sitting down and lecturing them after her own fashion—telling them of a fearful monster which had its abode beneath the water, or of wild men who lay concealed in the scrub ready to carry them off and eat them.   Poor Betty had no notion of

THE ARRIVAL OF THE BLACK " HELP "—(See p. 67).

right or wrong, and, although she did not steal or tell falsehoods, it was from the belief that the white people, who knew everything, would to a certainty find her out. As soon as she had obtained some knowledge of English, Mary and Janet endeavoured to instil into her dark mind some religious ideas. It was long, however, before they were satisfied that she had comprehended the simplest truths.

The family were now anxiously waiting Paul's return. All the flour in the store-room had been exhausted, but they were not so badly off as they might have been in some regions. The captain had an acre or more planted with the sweet potato—a species of yam, each root weighing from three to four pounds, and sometimes even more. Biddy had learned to cook them properly, when they appeared dry and floury. Though the cousins at first declared that they were too sweet to eat, they acknowledged, however, when dressed under the roast meat, that they were very nice. Then they had bananas, a pleasant, nutritious fruit. The captain, on first coming to the farm, had formed a plantation of these trees, and as they had been well protected they had escaped destruction from the hurricane. The trees were raised from suckers, which grew around the bottom of the parent tree. Within eighteen months from the time the plants had been set out the trees began to bear fruit. This comes out from the centre of the plant, and hangs down in a large bunch, five or six in a bunch.

One great advantage was that there were ripe bananas all the year round, though they were most plentiful in the summer. The trees were upwards of twenty feet in height, with broad green leaves four to six feet in length. There was an avenue composed of them running from one side of the garden to the other, which afforded at all times a delightful shade. The stems contain a quantity of fibrous matter, which makes excellent rope.

"We shall not starve while we have these to subsist on," observed the captain to his brother. "The people in the south call us 'Banana-men'; and not a bad name either, for with their aid we could manage to subsist on beef and mutton, even had we no other vegetable productions to depend upon."

Mary and Janet had nearly two hundred hens in their

poultry yard, and by attending carefully to them and not allowing them to stray, they were able to obtain several dozen eggs daily.

Hector and the younger boys frequently went out fishing, but Harry and Reggy preferred shooting. On one occasion Hector volunteered to accompany them.

The boys were feeling somewhat fatigued from their walk, when they reached a large water-hole, which they had not before visited.

" The water looks very refreshing; I intend to have a bath," said Hector, beginning to undress.

Just then Harry caught sight of a flight of parrots, which had pitched in some trees near at hand. Reginald and he crept near. Firing together they brought down nearly a dozen. They were picking up the birds when they heard Hector cry out. Running back to the water-hole, they saw him almost in the middle.

" Help me! help me ! " he shouted.

" Why, if you've got thus far, why can't you wade back again ? " asked Harry.

" There are some horrid creatures sticking to me, and I don't know what they will do," cried Hector.

Harry and Reggy, caring nothing for the wetting, plunged in, and soon helped Hector back on to dry ground. He had not cried out without reason, for what was their dismay to see twenty or thirty leeches sticking to his body, and several had fixed themselves to their own arms even during the short time they had been in the water. They pulled them off as fast as they could, but found it no easy matter to stop the blood which flowed from some of the spots to which the creatures had fixed themselves.

" I shall bleed to death! I shall bleed to death!" sighed poor Hector.

" I don't think things will be so bad as that," said Harry.

The leeches were very small at first, looking somewhat like thick bits of hair, but they rapidly began to swell, and two which stuck on Reggy's wrist, which he did not observe while assisting his brother, had grown to the size of his little finger. Fortunately the leeches were wiped off poor Hector's body before they had time to extract much of his blood. Although he declared that he felt very faint he soon recovered, and being attended to by Reggy and Harry, put on his clothes, vowing that it should be the last time he would ever bathe in that detestable country.

"All water-holes have not got leeches in them," observed Harry. "There are none in those near Stratton, and I would advise you to break that resolution."

Hector, however, declaring that he felt very ill, insisted on returning home.

"Any news of Paul yet?" asked Harry, as they arrived at home.

"Not a word," said his father; "if he does not appear to-morrow I intend to ride out and try to discover him."

Hector, meanwhile, was bitterly complaining to his mother of the sufferings he had endured. "I wish that you'd let me go back to England, or try and get me some gentlemanly post in Sydney or Melbourne," he said.

"I will ask your father," was the answer.

The captain, to whom Mr. Berrington communicated his son's request, laughed heartily. "I am sorry for the poor boy. He would find that he had dropped out of the frying-pan into the fire. If he cannot find occupation in the bush, depend upon it he will not in the city. People there do not want fine young gentlemen any more than they do here. Do not let him go, as you will only be throwing your money away, but have patience with him, and by degrees he will get accustomed to our ways, and prove useful at last."

Mr. Berrington told his son " that he would think about

the matter," and Hector used to talk to his cousins of the Government appointment he expected soon to obtain.

The heat had been very great. Not a cloud was in the sky, and not a breath of wind fanned the topmost boughs of the tallest trees. Captain Berrington had determined on starting to discover what had become of Paul. Rob and Edgar were awake before daylight. The whole family intended to be up to see the captain off. The window was left open on account of the heat. Presently, from the wood close at hand, there came forth a wild shriek of merry laughter, which made Hector start up.

"Where in the world did that come from?" he exclaimed.

Rob pointed to the wood.

"What can it be?" asked Hector.

Rob did not answer, amused at his cousin's astonishment.

Again, another jovial peal of laughter, followed by a self-satisfied chuckle, came from the wood.

"What is it? What is it?" asked the others.

"You would have heard it before, many a time, if you had been awake at this hour," answered Rob. "That is the settler's alarum—the laughing jackass."

"Laughing jackass!" exclaimed Hector. "I never heard that a jackass laughed, and I don't see one there," for in his eagerness he had jumped up, and gone to the window.

The dawn, it should have been said, had just broken.

"Wait until we have more light," said Rob; "perhaps you will then see our friend. I can just make him out. He is not down on the ground, where you are looking for him—he is up in yonder tree."

"Up in a tree?" exclaimed his cousins, in chorus.

"Yes; he generally lives up there, but he does not indulge in such uproarious laughter until early in the morning. I suppose he laughs at the folly of people lying in bed, and so tries to wake them up."

Hector and Edgar were more mystified than ever. At last they caught sight of a large brown bird with a big beak, sitting on a bough and nodding its head, and then laughing away with all its might. They could now no longer have any doubt whence the sound proceeded.

Just then Harry, arriving from the hut, came into the room.

"Come along, Harry," cried Reggy, "you said there would be time for a bathe before breakfast."

"I'm your man," said Harry. "Come, be quick, Hector, or we shall be back before you have put the finishing touch to your toilet."

The two lads hurried down to the river. Except in the water-holes which were joined by a trickling rivulet the whole bed was dry, but the ponds were of sufficient depth to afford a pleasant bath.

The boys were on the point of throwing off their clothes to plunge in, when Harry exclaimed, "Hark! what's that sound?"

"It is like distant thunder," answered Reggy.

"It can't be thunder, there's not a cloud in the sky," replied Harry. "It seems to me to be coming right down the river. I don't like it; I heard just such a sound some years ago, when a great flood came down and rose nearly up to the house. We won't bathe, but run back and tell father; he'll judge what it is and what's best to be done."

The boys hurried back; but before they had got up to the top of the bank the roaring sound had greatly increased, and Harry was more convinced than before that a heavy flood was approaching.

CHAPTER X.

Alarming Progress of the Flood—The Captain removes his Family to
higher ground—The Boys, in their eagerness to save more Property,
are cut off by the Water.

DIRECTLY on receiving the information brought by Harry and Reggy, Captain Berrington hurried down to the river, followed by Hector, Rob, and Edgar. Presently, as they looked up the dry bed between the high banks, they saw a wall of water moving on towards them, such, on a smaller scale, as might have been beheld by the Egyptians when attempting to cross the Red Sea. But this was high enough to overwhelm any human beings, or horses or cattle, which might have been in its way. The summit hissed and foamed, rising almost to the top of the bank. No streams advanced before it: it was literally a wall of water. On it came, its roar growing louder and louder In less than a minute after it had been seen it rushed by, filling the whole bed of the river, and sending its surges up those portions of the bank which sloped more gradually.

"Back, back, boys!" shouted the captain.

They had to run as quickly as their legs would carry them to avoid the torrent. Where the ground had just before been perfectly dry there was now a hissing, foaming torrent of yellow water, carrying along branches of trees, and even big trunks. The captain, who had been joined by his brother, watched it anxiously.

"I had hopes that this was merely the result of a thunder-storm up the country," he observed; "but see, it continues to rise, which shows me that there must be a vast volume of water behind what there is here. We have some cattle feeding on the low land higher up; I trust that White has had the discretion to drive them to the upper ground."

"I fear some animals have been caught, if not ours," observed Mr. Berrington. "There go the bodies of two heifers. See, here comes a third."

The captain was silent for a few minutes. "Harry!" he exclaimed, "run and tell Sandy to put the horses in all the drays, and bring them down here."

"What's that for?" asked Mr. Berrington, as Harry ran off to obey the order.

"The river once came up within three feet of the house. Had it risen a foot higher it would have flooded the whole ground. It may rise two, three, or four feet higher than that. I wish to be prepared for the worst, and to save what property we can, with our wives and children, in case the house should be flooded."

The captain desired all the party to return with him, and then announced his apprehensions to the ladies. "We will breakfast first, and then pack up the most valuable portion of our property, so that we may decamp if necessary," he said, calmly. His spirit inspired the rest: even Mrs. Berrington, who for a wonder had got up, ate some breakfast. The boys set to with a will.

"You know we may have some work to do, and it's wise to take in plenty of provender beforehand. We don't know when we may have time to eat again," observed Harry, cracking his third egg.

His brothers and cousins followed his example, in spite of the roaring sound which continued outside.

Biddy and Betty were busy packing up the cooking utensils, while the ladies were employed in filling their trunks with their clothes and the most valuable articles they possessed. Poor Mrs. Berrington's state can better be imagined than described. Her sister's time was much taken up in endeavouring to calm her alarm. The captain again went out. The river, as he feared would be the case, had greatly increased. Still, it might possibly not rise higher than it had done before. He stuck several poles in the ground to mark its progress. The first, then the second and the third, were reached with unexpected rapidity. Already the water was rushing over the opposite bank where the ground was lowest, sweeping everything before it There was a danger that the scrub being carried away might form a dam lower down, and, if so, create much greater damage than if the river continued open to its mouth.

"I wish the drays would come," the captain said to his brother. "We must get our wives and girls as soon as possible to the top of the ridge. I thank heaven this did not occur at night, or we might have been washed out of our beds."

Still Mr. Berrington could not believe that the water would come up higher.

"Look there!" said the captain, pointing to the southward among the trees; "it is flooding the whole scrub. In a short time this place will be surrounded."

As he spoke, two or three kangaroos and several wallabies were seen in the distance making their escape into the open.

"These fellows know there is danger, or they would not be going at that rate," observed the captain.

As the drays had not arrived, Reggy offered to set off to hurry them on.

"We intend to take you for a morning drive," exclaimed Mr. Berrington to his wife, in as cheerful a voice as he could command.

"But why should we leave the house?" she asked.

"Merely as a matter of precaution," answered the captain. "It is possible that the water may reach close up to us, and the ground between this and the ridge is lower, so that we should have a difficulty in crossing it should the house be flooded."

"Here come the drays," cried Rob, who had been looking out for them. Harry was driving one, Reggy another, and Bendigo a third. Sandy and the men had galloped off to gather in the cattle on the higher ground, and Bendigo and Harry had had a hard matter to put to the horses, which had caused the delay.

"There is no time to be lost now," whispered the captain to his brother. "We will load the drays as fast as we can. You shall drive your wife and mine, with the young children; the rest of us will follow as soon as we can."

Without a moment's delay the drays were loaded. Biddy and Betty, as Harry declared, "worked like troopers." The trunks and boxes having been put in, their bedding was placed on the top of them. Still there was all the furniture and various articles which it seemed a pity to leave to the mercy of the flood.

"You go on, father," cried Harry to the captain, "with the girls; Reggy, Hector, and I, with Biddy and the blacks,

will soon load up with a few more things and quickly overtake you."

The captain, who was anxious to place the girls in
safety, with a portion of their property, trusting to Harry's
discretion, followed his advice.

"Don't delay," he shouted, pointing to the water, which
was already overflowing the kitchen garden, though it had
not yet reached the road they were to cross. Hector was
ashamed to ask to go with the captain, though he would
infinitely rather have done so. He, indeed, exerted himself far more than he had ever been known to do before.

Biddy and Betty were as active as ever, carrying out
all sorts of things, some of which might have been left
behind, until Harry and Reggy pointed out what was
considered of most value. Already the dray was as full
as it could hold. Bendigo shouted out that it was time to
be off, and jumped on the seat.

"We go now, we go now!" he cried.

Biddy and Betty clung to the hinder part of the dray,
struggling in vain to get in.

"Off with you," exclaimed Harry; "we will follow on
foot."

Bendigo cracked his whip, and his horses dashed forward
at such a rate that it was a wonder the dray did not immediately capsize. Harry watched it anxiously as it went
down a dip from which there was a gentle rise. Already
a stream of water was running through the hollow, but it
looked a mere rivulet, not half a foot deep, which could
be passed over with a good spring.

"It is a pity we should not get a few more goods," said
Harry; "although I don't believe the water will reach
the house: yet, if it does, everything will be spoiled, if
not washed away."

They hurried through the rooms, picking up whatever
they thought most valuable. Even Hector was inspired

with a desire to save something, especially several articles belonging to himself. Harry had taken a run into the kitchen, where he discovered some dampers, which Biddy in her alarm had forgotten to remove from the ashes.

"It is a pity to lose these," said Harry, clapping them into the pockets of his jacket—good capacious ones, as every bushman's should be. There was, besides, a pot of yams, by this time completely cooked.

"Here, Reggy, stow some of these away," he cried out. "The chances are that we shall not have too much to eat on the top of the hill there, unless Biddy has been more thoughtful than she appears to have been when she left these. What she could have been about I don't know!"

So busily were they engaged that they did not hear the increased roar of the waters.

"Come, you fellows, it's time to be off, I'm sure," cried Hector, who had been feeling very nervous all the time.

"Just half a minute longer," answered Harry; "I must lash these things up."

Hector, however, would not stop, and rushed out of the house. Directly afterwards he came back, looking very pale.

"The water is rushing through the hollow like a mill-sluice!" he exclaimed; "we shall lose our lives if we attempt to cross."

Harry and Reggy followed him out. He spoke too truly. They were cut off from what was now the mainland by a foaming torrent twelve yards or more in width, which was carrying along fruit trees, rocks, and palings, whirling them round and round so that it would be impossible to swim across or to wade, even should the depth allow of their doing so. Hector threw down his load and wrung his hands.

"Stay!" cried Harry, "we've got a ladder! we may get across by that."

They all three ran back for it, and attempted to throw it across, but the channel was too wide, and it was almost torn from their grasp. It would have been lost had not Harry fastened a rope to the lower round, by which it was hauled in.

"The ladder may be useful for another purpose," observed Harry.

They lifted it up and carried it back to the house. The water was by this time rising even faster than before. The maize field, the yam and potato-ground, the orchard and kitchen-garden, were all flooded. Palings and hedges were everywhere giving way before the torrent. A rise of another foot would bring it up to the walls of the house. The floor was somewhat higher, so that it would not damage that much should the flood cease to rise when it got thus far. But would it cease? was the question. If it once began to beat against the walls of the house, would they stand? Reggy proposed climbing up to the roof by means of the ladder.

"That would be a place of very doubtful safety," said Harry.

They looked up the stream, now extending a quarter of a mile or more on either side of its original bed. The whole country around them seemed flooded, with the exception of the hill to which the drays had gone.

"I am afraid that it will reach the stock-yard," said Harry, "and it must be close to it already; if so, the cattle will have a poor chance. See, it has already carried away the hen-house, and there go the poor hens, flying away towards the nearest branches they can reach. Unfortunately, I cut the wings of a number only the other day because they would stray, and now they will all be lost."

"Oh! what shall we do? What shall we do?" exclaimed Hector.

"We are not going to lose our lives if we can help it," said Harry, who retained his presence of mind.

He was just then watching the piggeries. The torrent struck them, carrying away the palings and letting the inmates loose.

"Foolish beasts!" exclaimed Harry, "instead of swimming towards the shore they are going with their heads down the stream, taking it quite coolly. They might have been on dry ground in five minutes if they had gone in the right direction."

Notwithstanding Harry's warning, Hector insisted on getting upon the roof.

"The water would surely not rise much above the floor, and as the house had withstood the hurricane it would not be knocked down by the flood," he said.

Calling to Reggy to help him, he climbed up and took his seat on the ridge.

"Come up! come up!" he shouted to Harry and Reggy; "you will be safe enough here."

"You had better come down and get up that tree," answered Harry, pointing to one which stood on ground of the same level as the house, and but a short distance from it.

Besides its trunk there were the numerous pendants, which had struck down and taken root, so that it was more likely to resist the torrent than any other of the trees near.

Hector, however, was obstinate. He was confident that he was safe, at all events for the present, and thought he should remain so.

"I should grow giddy if I were to climb up into such a tree as that," he answered; "Reggy, you may go if you like, but I'll stay here."

Harry, who carried the ladder, placed it against the tree, which reached sufficiently high to enable them to

get hold of one of the lower branches, by which they
could hoist themselves higher.   Harry, however, had no
intention of going up until it became absolutely necessary.
Still the water rose. It was now sweeping over the ground
on which they stood.   Reggy, again entreating Hector to
come, rushed up to the tree and mounted the ladder. Just
then the captain and Mr. Berrington appeared in the dis-

"THEY MADE TOWARDS THE LADDER "—(*See* p. 83).

tance. The roar of the waters prevented their voices
being heard. Their alarm at seeing their boys placed in
so perilous a position was, of course, very great. Harry
saw them making signs and pointing to the tree.

"They want you to do as I advise," shouted Harry.
"Come down ! come down ! "

Hector felt the house shake, as a surge beat against it

larger than any of its predecessors.　He lost confidence in the safety of his position.

"Slip off the roof by the verandah," shouted Harry.

At length, as he saw Harry still standing below him, not being aware that the water was over his ankles, he slid down.

When Hector discovered that he must jump into the water, he attempted to climb back again. This, however, from his alarm, and from being unaccustomed to climb, was more than he could do, and down he slid, Harry catching him at the bottom.

"Now run for it!" cried the latter, seizing him by the arm, and they made towards the ladder, the water hissing and foaming at their heels.

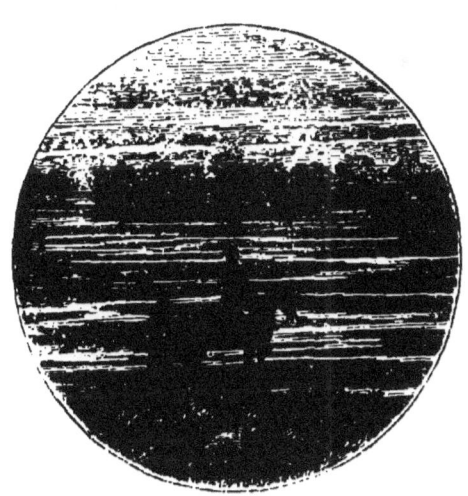

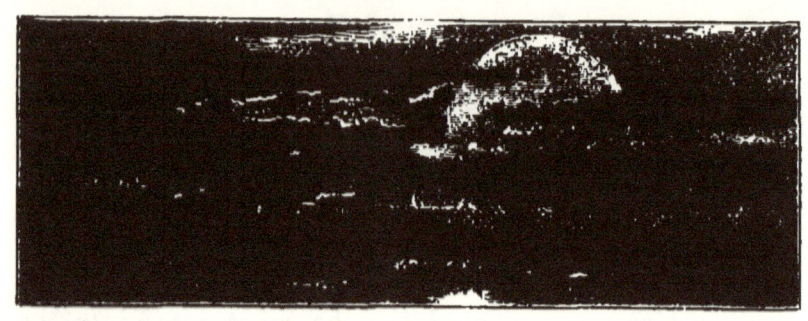

CHAPTER XI.

The Boys take refuge in a Tree—The House carried away—Destruction of Cattle—A Cow caught in the Boughs—A Night up the Tree—Harry keeps up the Spirit of the Party.

THE flood came roaring up, carrying everything in its course on either side of the ground over which the lads were making their way. Hector had begun to cry out when he saw how high the water was.

"It won't wash us away yet, never fear," exclaimed Harry, dragging him along. It was almost up to their knees, however, before they reached the ladder. "You go up first," said Harry. "Be quick about it; I'll follow."

Hector began to climb the ladder much slower than

Harry liked, for as he looked round he saw a huge wave, far wider, though not so high as that which first appeared, roaring and leaping as it came down the river. Trees and fences, which had hitherto withstood the flood, gave way before it.

"Quick, quick," cried Harry, shoving Hector up, "it will be upon us in a few seconds, and may carry the ladder away."

On it came, surging up against the walls of the house. Reggy caught hold of Hector's hand and handed him up on the branch.

"We must get higher up than this," he shouted; "look there! look there!"

Harry again turned round. The house seemed literally to melt away before the flood. The water rose around it, and then, as the wave rushed on, the fragments of the walls and roof were seen floating on mixed with articles of furniture, chairs, tables, and bedsteads. Now the wave surged against the tree. Harry had just time to spring on to the branch, and to secure the ladder by a rope when the lower end was lifted, and it would have been carried away by the flood had it not thus fortunately been secured. The lads watched the various articles as they floated by, hopelessly lost, for in a few minutes they would be driven by the current against the trunks of trees, or the rocks, and would be dashed to pieces.

By climbing out to the end of a branch Harry was able to see where his father and uncle were standing, and to make a signal to them that he and his cousins were safe. This must greatly have relieved the mind of the captain and his brother, though they probably still considered the lads in greater danger than they themselves were inclined to believe that they were.

Several trees had been uprooted and carried along by the torrent, and theirs might share the same fate. Harry

returned again to the end of the branch, and found that
his father and uncle had gone away to look after the
party on the hill.

Harry now proposed that they should get higher
up, for the water had already risen several feet above
the ground, and might in a short time be up to the
branch in which they sat. Higher and higher they
got.

"When is it going to stop?" cried Reggy. "Harry,
do you think this is such a flood as that which drowned
all mankind except Noah's family?"

"I'm very sure it is not," answered Harry. "God
promised never to send such another, and put His bow in
the clouds as a token. I have heard of many such floods
in this country, though this, to be sure, is higher than
any we have known, and I cannot account for it; but I
have not the slightest doubt that it will stop before long,
though no doubt it will have done a great deal of damage.
That cannot be helped. It might have come on at night,
and we might all have been washed away before we knew
where we were, or fifty other things might have happened. We have reason to be thankful, as matters might
have been worse."

"I don't see how that could be," cried Hector. "To
have to take refuge in a tall tree, cut off from all help,
without anything to eat or drink, is as bad as one can
well conceive."

"Come, come, don't grumble; it never makes a person
happy, though it is said there are some fellows who are
never happy unless they are grumbling, but I don't
believe that."

"But if the flood does not subside before night, where
are we to sleep?" asked Hector.

"Why, up in the boughs, like birds or 'possums, to be

"... ...ED THE VARIOUS ARTICLES AS THEY FLOATED BY"—(see p. 85).

sure," answered Harry. "By-the-bye, we may find a
'possum, and he may serve us for supper."

"But how can we get a fire to cook him?" inquired
Reggy, with a slight suspicion that Harry was quizzing
his brother.

"Oh, as to that, we must eat him raw; but many a
sailor, wrecked on a desert island, has had to live on
worse fare," said Harry.

"Oh, dear! Oh, dear! I wish we had never come
out to this horrible country. We shall be starved, to a
certainty," moaned Hector; "I'm desperately hungry
already."

"Are you? Poor fellow! then you will have to come
to 'possum, or have to eat a tree-lizard, or our friend the
laughing jackass, or her eggs, if she happen to have a
nest in this tree. We must set off on a voyage of dis-
covery directly."

"I wonder you can joke, placed in so fearful a position
as we are," said Hector, in an angry tone.

"What would be the use of moaning and sighing, I
should like to know?" asked Harry. "I always like to
make the best of things. The flood won't last for ever.
It is sure to go down in two or three days or a week at
the most, and in the meantime we must make ourselves
comfortable where we are."

"Comfortable, indeed! up a fig-tree with nothing to
eat," groaned Hector.

"Well, well, old fellow, things are not so bad as that.
Here's a bit of damper to stay your appetite until we
can catch a 'possum or a laughing jackass for dinner;"
and Harry produced one of the dampers which he had
stowed away in his pocket.

This somewhat consoled Hector, who had hitherto
declared that he could never touch such doubgy stuff,
although he ate his share eagerly, as did Reggy his.

"It may be a satisfaction for you to know that I have got some more," said Harry; "but it won't do to eat them all up at once; we must put ourselves on an allowance, or we may have to starve at last. Now let us see how things are getting along."

Harry looked out from the leafy covert in which the three lads had ensconced themselves high up among the forks of the huge tree. The flood was still surging on, setting towards the south-east, and spreading farther and farther over the country. He was grieved to see a number of bullocks floating by, showing that the flood must be sweeping over some of the pastures, and have carried them off before they could be driven on to the higher ground. They were in all probability his father's. Their loss must inevitably be very heavy. Their house and the greater part of their furniture was gone. How many heads of cattle he could not calculate. Other settlers farther down must have suffered in the same degree, perhaps in a still greater.

"We ought to be thankful that the lives of all the family have been saved, and three drays full of property. If father hadn't been wide awake, they would have been lost too," said Harry. At last he caught sight of some pigs feeding on the shore. "Well, those fellows have saved themselves, at all events, and I see some hens, too, in those trees; well, matters might be worse, we must acknowledge that."

Reggy agreed with him, but nothing would comfort Hector; his only remark was that—"It is a horrible, detestable country; if I can once get out of it I won't come back in a hurry."

> "Three little blackbirds sat in a tree—
> Singing, heigh-ho, heigh-ho, fiddle-de-dee,"

sang Harry. "Now I vote we make a nest for ourselves;

as to the water sinking low enough to allow our getting on shore to-night, that's out of the question. Come, Reggy, help me up with the ladder, we must not let that go; we may find it useful in getting down some day or other, and the rope will help to make our nest."

They hauled up the ladder and placed it horizontally across the boughs.

"Stay," cried Harry, "if we get it up into this fork it will serve as a back to our sleeping-place, and the rope passed two or three times backwards and forwards will secure the sides." Harry had his axe in his belt. "We must cut some boughs to raise the sides, lest we should stray in our sleep and tumble overboard."

By creeping along one of the boughs they were able to reach some small branches suited to their purpose. These were secured by means of some of the fine vines which hung about the boughs. Harry and Reggy declared the nest they had formed was perfect.

"I vote we have an annual feast here in commemoration of this flood," said Harry, "and we will invite our friends to join us."

"It will hold all who come," growled Hector. "I would rather try to forget so disagreeable an event."

"There are some fellows who are never satisfied," said Harry, looking away from Hector.

Harry did his best to keep up his cousins' spirits and his own by talking away. Their conversation was interrupted by feeling some heavy body strike the tree, and looking down they saw a bullock, which had come down the torrent, driven against some of the lower branches, on which the poor animal was endeavouring to find a foot-hold; it succeeded, and remained fixed in the boughs. Its struggles soon ceased, and it was pretty clear that, overcome by its exertions, it was dead, for its head hung over the boughs into the water.

"No fear of starving," said Harry; "we may have as much beef-steak as we like."

"Thank you! I'd rather not eat such horrid stuff," said Hector.

"As you please," answered Harry. "The time may come when you will change your tone."

Night was approaching, the water was evidently rising less rapidly than before, still it was spreading over the country. Here and there hillocks and knolls appeared like islands in the midst of the sea.

"I wish that we had brought a gun with us, we could have made a signal to our friends that we are all safe. My fear is that they will be anxious about us." Harry did not for a moment think about himself. "Well, old fellows, it's time to turn in."

After they had finished their frugal supper of damper and sweet potatoes they arranged themselves for the night.

"Don't take to walking in your sleep, Hector, and you'll be all right," said Harry.

"But what if the tree should give way! I'm certain I felt it shake," groaned Hector.

"Cling to the boughs like grim death," answered Harry; "it won't sink, and we shall be floated to shore somehow or other."

CHAPTER XII.

THE darkness of the night contributed to make the position of the three lads even more trying than it had been during the day. Notwithstanding Harry's assertions, even Reggy could not help fearing that the tree might be carried away. The roar of the waters did not for a moment cease, while the wind howled through the branches, and the occasional lowing of some heifers more fortunate than their companions, and who had landed on some island knoll, reached their ears. The stout tree, however, held firm, and after some hours' anxious watching they all dropped off to sleep. They were awakened by a loud cheerful cachination close above their heads, and on looking up, what should they see but their friend the laughing jackass, looking very much surprised to find them in such near proximity to its mate's nest.

" Much obliged to you, old fellow," said Harry to the

bird, which nodded its head in response, and laughed again as if he were going to split his sides.

"That's a good sign," observed Harry; "there's no storm coming, or he would not be so merry. It's my belief that we shall find the water has dropped considerably."

Harry was right, for on looking down they saw the unfortunate bullock hanging in the branches considerably above the surface, while the force of the current was evidently much lessened. The water, indeed, at the first glance seemed to be sinking into the earth, but, watching more narrowly, they could detect currents running from all quarters into the main stream, which still went hissing and foaming on as before.

They all felt very thirsty, but none of them were inclined to drink the muddy liquid which flowed by them. At last they could hold out no longer, and Harry, unreeving the rope, descended to the water and brought up a hatful. It did not look nearly as yellow as they had expected, and they were thankful to quench their thirst. The day wore on.

"If no further flood comes down, I really believe that we may be able to get on shore to-night," said Harry.

"I hope so, indeed," moaned Hector; "to have to sleep again up among the boughs would be terrible; my back aches fearfully."

Harry proved to be mistaken, for when darkness returned the water was still too deep to allow of their making their way to the hill where they hoped to find their family, especially as they could not tell what channels and holes might have been formed by the torrent. They had still enough damper and sweet potato to last them for another meal.

They were again awakened by that irrepressible fellow, the laughing jackass, at early dawn, and on looking out from their leafy bower they found that the ground beneath their feet was dry.

" Now let us get down and make the best of our way to the hill, to let our fathers and mothers know we are safe," he exclaimed. They soon reached the ground. To walk over it, however, was not very easy, as it was thickly covered with slime. Not a vestige of the house remained, nor a fence of any sort. The whole land had been reduced to a perfect wilderness.

" It is ours still, however," observed Harry, " and will probably prove twice as fruitful as it was before, and won't require manuring for years to come. I dare say father will think of that, and it will be some consolation to him. Now, let's move on."

This was more easily said than done. They attempted to walk steadily, but, instead, went slipping and sliding about, and in some places they could with difficulty make progress. They had not gone far when they caught sight of Mr. Hayward. He expressed his delight at seeing them.

" We have indeed been anxious about you, though the captain was satisfied that you were safe," exclaimed their tutor.

On getting off the ground which had been covered with water, the boys hurried on, and soon reached the hill, on the side of which, under a grove of acacia-trees, they found the family encamped. The tent which had been stowed at the station had been put up for the accommodation of the ladies, while the rest of the party slept either in or under the drays. They had not in reality suffered much hardship, as they were as well off as they would have been in making a journey, with the exception of want of bread.

Mrs. Hugh and her daughters were making the best of everything, though it was sad for them to contemplate the fruitful spot amid which their house had stood, now a slimy wilderness.

"Any news of Paul?" asked Harry.

Captain Berrington shook his head. "I am thankful I had not started from home when this occurred; but I must now try and learn what has become of him," he answered. "Should he have escaped all other dangers, he may have been caught by this flood; and I am indeed very, very anxious."

Harry told Mr. Hayward what his father had said.

"I am ready to start this instant, either alone or with any one whom your father will allow to accompany me," he said.

"I'll go!" cried Harry.

"You may be wanted; there is work to do for all hands, though perhaps I can best be spared," answered Mr. Hayward.

Thinking that Bendigo might be useful in learning from any blacks they might meet if Paul's drays had been seen, he asked whether he would go.

Bendigo replied that he was quite ready. Harry, also, to his great satisfaction got leave to accompany his tutor.

As the horses were quite fresh, and the saddles had been saved, they agreed to start immediately; though they would have to trust to their guns for provisions, except when they could fall in with any sheep-stations, where beef and mutton could be procured.

Everywhere as they rode along were signs of the destruction caused by the flood.

"It must be a lesson to us and others not to build near one of these rivers, liable to such inundations," said Mr. Hayward. "Had not your father possessed cattle and sheep, he would have been ruined; as it is, he has suffered severe loss. But how admirably does he and your mother bear it, as they do the prolonged absence of Paul. It raises them more than ever in my estimation. I hope we shall be fortunate in finding a satisfactory spot for a new location, as he will not be again tempted to build in his old one. I believe if Paul is restored to them safe, they will look upon their losses as trifles."

This conversation occurred on the second day of their journey. They had just mounted a slight ridge, and before them spread out a wide extent of level land.

" I think I see something very like a dray, with two horsemen near it," said Harry.

Mr. Hayward could not make out the objects which his young companion's sharp eyes had detected; still they both instinctively increased their speed.

" I'm sure it is a dray, with a man on horseback. The dray is very like ours, and the rider like Paul. Hurrah ! " cried Harry, and putting spurs to his horse he dashed forward.

Mr. Hayward followed, although not quite as fast, and saw Harry shaking hands with the stranger ; and even he was soon convinced that the first of the two was Paul.

After the first greetings were over, and they were once more moving towards Stratton, Paul described how he had been attacked by bush-rangers, whom he had beaten off, and his narrow escape from the flood.

Paul, as may be supposed, was received with joyful welcome by the family.

The first thing to be done was to build a house for the ladies, where they might be secure should another inundation occur. The captain, however, was of opinion that that was not at all likely, as the late one was higher than had ever been known to take place by the oldest colonists. Towards the proposed work all hands devoted the whole of their energies ; and hewing, sawing, and carrying of timber went on from morning until night.

In little more than a week, a tolerably substantial house of a size sufficient to hold the ladies of the family was put up, but some days more were required to manufacture bedsteads, chairs, tables, and other articles of furniture. However, within a fortnight the family were once more settled, and a stranger visiting them would not have supposed how a short time before they had been houseless.

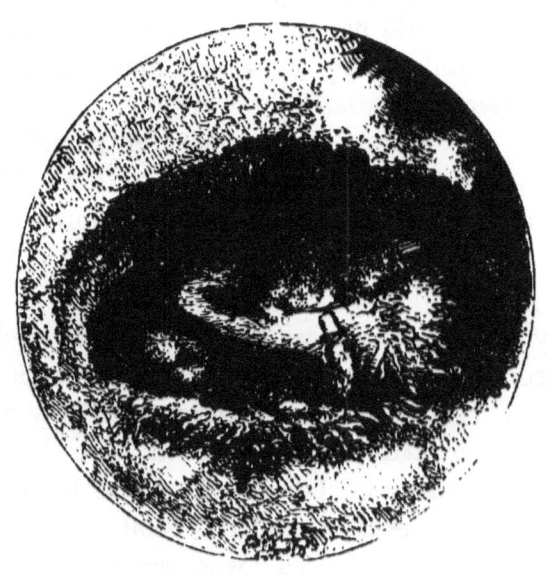

CHAPTER XIII.

THE captain was anxious to commence, without a moment's delay, his proposed exploring expedition. He intended to form two parties, so as to inspect a large tract of country in a short time. Naturally, his brother would have taken one, and he the other; but Mr. Berrington was so little accustomed to bush-life, that the captain persuaded him to remain at home, and to let Mr. Hayward lead the other party.

Hector, who had no great liking for Mr. Hayward, begged that he might accompany his uncle.

Sandy would have liked to follow his master, but his duties kept him at home.

"Mr. Berrington is a verra gude gentleman, but he kens little about farm-work as yet, and I canna trust him." he observed.

The captain took the most trustworthy of the men, thus making up his party to four. Paul, Harry, and Reggy accompanied Mr. Hayward, and with the addition of Bendigo, who was likely to prove very useful, their party was complete.

They were all well mounted, Paul having Old Bolter to ride. Their equipment was simple in the extreme. They each carried their rifles and pistols, with a good supply of ammunition, small shot and bullets, axes and long knives, a blanket to sleep in at night, and a tin pannikin; while between them they had a kettle for boiling water, a camp oven, two large canvas water-bags, a store of tea, salt and pepper, some flour in a bag, with a thick piece of canvas for kneading it, while sugar and all other luxuries were dispensed with.

Their dresses were red shirts, thick duck trousers, broad-brimmed hats, blucher boots, and leggings, with a strap round the waist to hold the axe and pouch containing matches, knife, and other small articles. Their course was to be towards the west and north-west. The first four or five days they were to travel together, after this they were to separate, the captain keeping a little to the northward of west and then circling round to the southward; and Mr. Hayward travelling to the southward of west and circling round to the northward; and then to return towards the spot from whence they had started. They would thus explore a wide extent of country, and would, they hoped, find a suitable spot for forming a fresh location.

The boys were in high spirits, forgetting all their previous troubles. The expedition they were undertaking was exactly what they had often talked about doing alone, without any grown-up person. However, Mr. Hayward always made himself so completely one of them that they were glad of his society.

The country they passed over during the first two days they were well acquainted with, and they met with no adventures. The first night they stopped at a hut on their most remote out-station. Beyond this they reached a lofty range, on the opposite side of which their explorations were to commence. As it rose in the distance it appeared to be no formidable barrier, but as they got near, lofty cliffs or precipices, and steep slopes covered with brushwood, seemed to rise out of the plain, such as must present an almost insuperable obstacle to the progress of the horses. Hector declared that no human being could surmount them.

"We must get up somehow or other, and with our horses too," answered Captain Berrington, laughing.

In a short time they found a dry channel down which a torrent had made its way, and by this they proceeded, still keeping in their saddles. At length, however, they had to dismount to climb a steep slope among rocks and trees. Now they turned to the right, now to the left, now they had to descend a shoulder of the mountain, now to ascend again, the captain carefully marking the way by barking the trees, or, where there were no trees, by piling up fragments of rocks.

The eastern was fortunately the worst side of the range. The descent on the west side down a moderate slope brought them into an undulating park-like plain, covered with grass sprinkled over with the ever-present blue and white gum-trees, while just before them appeared an open patch of green plain, offering a tempting feed to cattle.

Smoke ascending from two or three shepherds' huts in the distance showed that this part of the country was already occupied. They had, therefore, to proceed until they could reach an unclaimed district. The last night the party were together they camped in a wood on the borders of a river in which, though its course was dry, there were several water-holes within half a mile of each other.

As they had ridden on all day without water for the horses they halted early. The captain, however, would not allow a fire to be lighted until nightfall, lest its smoke might attract the attention of the blacks, who, although they might not venture to attack them, would watch their future movements, and perhaps, if unfriendly, cause them some annoyance.

At night there would be less risk of a fire being seen, unless by any one coming close up to the camp, providing the flames were not allowed to ascend to any great height. The horses, as usual, were hobbled near, and they were sure not to stray away from the good grass and water.

As usual, the captain and Paul, who were the best shots of the party, took their guns to provide supper and break-fast, no difficult task, as parrots, pigeons, and other birds abounded. They brought back an ample supply, with the addition of a wallaby and a bandicoot. The larger portion of the latter animals would serve as a supper for the dogs. The boys had taken off the edge of their appetites with some cold damper, which they had brought in their pouches, and some wild fruit they had met with, but were very glad when the captain allowed them at last to light the pile of sticks they had collected, to put on the kettle, and to begin roasting the game. Harry and Reggy undertook to make some fresh dampers, Paul to attend to the camp oven, while Hector was set to turn the spits. The rest of the party were clearing the ground round the fire, bringing water, looking after the horses, and putting up some slabs of bark to serve as a shelter for the night. All hands were "as busy as bees," as Harry remarked.

Supper over—the last they expected to take together

for some weeks—most of the party prepared for rest.
The fire was allowed to smoulder, but no fresh sticks were
put on, and they believed that even should any natives be
in the neighbourhood they would not have discovered
the camp.

Harry proposed, before turning in, taking a bath in
another water-hole, a short distance down the bed of the
river, as they did not quite like the idea of bathing in
the one from which they were to fill their kettle and
water-bottles the next morning. The sun had only just
disappeared, though darkness was rapidly coming on.
However, there was the moon which would enable them
to see their way. They could not possibly lose it by
returning along the bank of the river; but as the scrub
was tolerably open and the ground hard, they settled to
make their way through it instead of trudging over the
soft sand in the bed of the stream.

They had got near the water-hole when they saw a
number of small lights moving among the trunks of the
trees, now appearing, now disappearing.

" Why, those must be fire-flies," cried Reggy.

" They are far too red and bright for that," whispered
Paul; "don't speak above your breath. The lights come
from the fire-sticks carried by natives, they always move
about with them by night, and they are gathering round
the water-hole. See! there are others coming from an
opposite direction, they are either going to have a cor-
robberee or a fight, perhaps both; we must take care not
to be discovered. They are so intent on what they are
about, however, that they are not likely to observe
us."

" I should like to see what they are going to do," said
Reggy. "We need not retreat, I suppose? "

"Oh, no! let us stop," said Harry. " They will not
find us out if we keep quiet."

"We had better be off," remarked Hector, somewhat alarmed ; "they may knock us all on the head."

"No, no," replied Harry, "we have our arms, and we

AN AUSTRALIAN NATIVE.

are not going to run away from a few blacks ; I vote we stay and see what is going forward."

Paul consented, though he felt it would be more

prudent to return to the camp and warn their friends of the neighbourhood of the natives.

Concealed by some low bushes they remained where they were, and could see all that was going forward. Suddenly all was dark, but the sound of the natives' voices showed that they were still near where they had first been seen. Presently bright flames burst up from the ground—a fire had been lighted, but no one could be seen.

" They are between us and the fire," whispered Paul.

" I hope they are not coming this way," said Hector.

" No fear of that," answered Harry.

A minute elapsed, when Hector uttered an exclamation in a voice so loud that it was a wonder it did not betray them.

" Oh, look there! look there! what can those horrid things be ? "

As he spoke, at the opposite side of the fire there appeared what looked exactly like a band of dancing skeletons leaping and twisting in the most grotesque fashion. At the same time wild shrieks, cries, and shouts rose from a hundred voices, intended to represent singing, accompanied by the rattling of musical instruments, and the slapping of their parchment-like skins by the older natives rose in the night air. Now all the legs on one side would go up, now those on the other, now the arms would be thrown above the grinning skulls, now they would be placed akimbo, now they would sink close to the ground with bended knees, now spring up into the air. Indeed, they assumed in succession every possible attitude, all moving together as if pulled by one string. Then, as suddenly as they had appeared, they vanished from sight.

Reggy was on the point of crying out when Paul put his hand on his mouth.

"Can those be real skeletons?" inquired Hector.

"Oh, dear, no!" whispered Paul; "they are merely blacks who have painted their bodies in that curious fashion. They are holding one of their corrobberees. They will keep it up all night, and little rest we shall get while they are howling and shrieking in this fashion."

The boys, however, remained some time watching the strange, weird scene. It would be difficult to describe the various antics performed by the savages. So amused were the lads that they forgot how time passed; but Paul at length suggested that they should find their way back. It was no easy matter to do so through the thick wood, although they were assisted in steering their course by the noise behind them. At last they reached the bank of the river, when they were able to make better progress. They found the captain and the rest of the party very anxious about them. The noise of the natives had reached the camp, and it was feared that they might have fallen into their hands. Bendigo advised that they should start before daybreak.

"Black fellow sleep then; no come after us," he said.

The captain resolved to follow Bendigo's advice, but not to separate until they had proceeded some little way farther westward; so that the blacks, when they should discover their trail, would be influenced by the number of persons forming the party, and not venture to follow them.

A strict watch was, of course, kept during the night. Paul, his brother, and cousins, notwithstanding the noise, slept like tops. At the hour proposed the horses were caught and the party mounted.

The explorers crossed the bed of the river some way to the north, at a distance from the blacks' camp, and, as the ground was level, were able to make good progress. At noon they stopped at a water-hole, which, though very

" WATCHING THE STRANGE WEIRD SCENE."

muddy, enabled them to give a draught to their horses; but, unless it could be filtered, they felt no inclination to drink it themselves, their water-bottles being full. A fire was lighted, and some pigeons and other birds shot and cooked.

The two parties now separated, the captain pointing out the course Mr. Hayward was to take, while he struck more to the northward. What adventures might they not encounter before they again met!

CHAPTER XIV.

THE captain's party was soon
lost sight of. The boys rode
on in high spirits. In spite of the
heat the air felt pure and bracing.
The scenery for miles, however,
was unvarying—everywhere the
same gigantic gum-trees were to
be seen; but vast as were their
limbs, they afforded but little
shade. Some were scathed and
leafless, from others hung in tatters long strips of bark,
giving them a peculiar, ragged appearance. In the evening
they reached the hut of a shepherd. On account of the
blacks there were two hut-keepers, sturdy fellows, well-
armed. They said that further west there were no other
white men, and as they themselves had never been more
than a few miles from their hut in that direction they knew
nothing of the country, but that there was a water-hole at
the extreme limit of the station in the direction the
explorers were proceeding. It was full, the shepherd said,

when he was last there, but he could give them no other information. He and his mate would be very happy to accommodate them for the night; but Mr. Hayward, after surveying the interior of the hut, replied that he and his party would not incommode them, but would be content to sleep round their own camp fire, under a neighbouring tree. Tea, damper, and mutton were, however, plentifully supplied by their hosts.

Roused next morning by a laughing jackass, who had conveniently perched himself on a bough overhead, they took breakfast in the hut with the shepherd, and set off at the time he drove out his flock to pasture.

"I am very much afraid we shall be disappointed after all," said Paul, as they approached the water-hole.

"Why?" asked Reggy.

"Because I see no cockatoos, laughing jackasses, or other birds flying about. If there were water they would be there."

Paul's fears were realized—there was not a drop of water in the hole.

"Patience," cried Paul; "we shall probably fall in with another before night."

The poor horses, however, suffered more than their riders, as they had still some water in their canvas bottles. They rested for a time in the shade under the trees round the water-hole, and then again rode on. They were now in a perfectly new country. They kept their eyes about them on every side to discover such a region as they were in search of. They passed through a country which might have suited their purpose, but there was a great drawback—the want of water. That was absolutely necessary for either a sheep or cattle station. They rode on and on, their horses began to droop their heads; all that could be done was to moisten the poor animals' lips with a little water from the bottles.

"What would I not give for a large, juicy water-melon?" exclaimed Harry.

"Don't talk about such a thing," said Reggy; "still I shouldn't mind a few bunches of grapes."

"They are sour enough now," observed Paul; "but cheer up, the trees look thicker, and we shall come on water soon, or I am very much mistaken."

Mr. Hayward had spoken but little during the day. The boys observed that he was not in his usual spirits; though he did not complain, he was evidently ill. As the day advanced he grew worse, and Paul would have proposed stopping had they found water, but it would be out of the question to camp without it. Bendigo had never been in this part of the country, as he belonged to a tribe which inhabited a region to the east, until the white man came and drove them farther into the interior. The signs of water, however, should there be any in the neighbourhood, were not likely to escape his observation. He frequently stood up in his stirrups to look about him, but each time shook his head, observing, "No water here."

For several hours the poor horses had not tasted a drop, while they themselves had had barely sufficient to wet their lips. They were more likely to find it by going straight on than by turning either to the right hand or to the left. So on they went.

The day was drawing to a close, not a sign of water appeared, when suddenly Bendigo shouted, "Dare, dare!" and pointed to some trees which could be just seen in the horizon.

They pushed on, but on reaching the trees, the hollow in which water once had been was dry. A chorus of groans escaped the explorers. "On, on!" cried Paul. "We must not despair, we can hold out a few hours longer."

The moon got up, and, relieved from the heat of the sun, the explorers were better able to endure the want of water. Mile after mile they went on, their weary horses, however, moving but slowly. At length Paul cried out, "My beast seems to fancy that water is near; I feel him tugging at the rein."

"So does mine," said Harry.

"SUDDENLY BENDIGO SHOUTED 'DARE, DARE!'"

Bruce gave a bark, signifying his satisfaction, and dashed on. A silver spot appeared ahead, lighted by the beams of the moon, which had now risen high in the sky. The horses galloped on, Bruce dashed forward, Mr. Hayward seemed to revive. They reached a large water-hole! It was necessary to keep back the horses, however, lest they should rush in and stir up the mud. Paul and Harry dismounted, and while Bendigo took charge of their horses, they, unstrapping their pannikins, hurried down the bank. It was no easy matter to fill them, as they had to go down the bank, and then to wade through the mud to get to the water, which looked so bright at a distance.

"Take care that there are no leeches," said Mr. Hayward.

Paul had a piece of linen through which he strained the water from one pannikin to another, then handed it to Harry, who carried it to their tutor before he would touch any himself. Reggy was next served, then Harry, and Paul drank last. How delicious the liquid tasted.

"I could drink a dozen pannikins full," said Harry, as he drained off a second.

"So could I—two dozen, for that matter," said Reggy.

Paul had, therefore, no sinecure in filling the pannikins. Bruce had in the meantime quenched his thirst.

At last, as Harry said, "having taken off the edge of their thirst," Bendigo and the horses might now drink. The steeds were then hobbled, and preparations made for camping.

Bendigo said that he did not think any black fellows were in the neighbourhood, as he could discover no traces of them near the edges of the water-hole. None of the rest of the party could have pronounced an opinion on the subject.

The moon shone brightly over the ground, the fire was lighted, and damper and tea quickly made, while some birds which they had shot in the morning, and had been carried hung to their saddles, were speedily cooked.

During the night Mr. Hayward grew so much worse that Paul thought he was going to die. To advance, with the risk of not finding water the next day, would be madness. Paul suggested that they should go back to the hut, and leave him with the shepherd, while they went forward to meet the captain, who would otherwise become alarmed at not seeing them.

Mr. Hayward agreed to this, though he expressed a hope that he might sufficiently recover to be able to accompanying them. " We will wait here a day, however, and see how I am. After a short rest I may be strong enough to go forward."

During the day Paul and Harry shot several birds and pigeons, three ducks and a couple of wallabies. While Reginald sat by Mr. Hayward, Bendigo wandered about in search of fruits and roots, which none but a black would have discovered. When well boiled the latter served instead of potatoes, while the wild fruits were very refreshing. They had thus an abundant and varied fare.

Mr. Hayward did not appear to get better. They had come away without medicines, no one dreaming of being ill; still Paul hoped that their tutor would be sufficiently recovered to continue the journey the following morning : but when the time came, it was evident that he was not in a fit state to run the risk of having no good water to drink. They determined therefore to go back together, though two days would thus be lost. By starting at sunrise they made good progress during the cooler hours. Having filled their water-bottles they had enough to last them during the day, and to wet the lips of the horses and Bruce.

It was not until nightfall that they got back to the shepherd's hut. The men promised to take every possible care of Mr. Hayward, who, though not much worse, was certainly not better. He assured his young companions that he should recover in the course of a few days. " At all events, do not fail to come and look for me on your return," he said, smiling. "I should not like to be left here longer than is necessary."

They remained only during the night, and again starting before the sun rose they reached the water-hole where they had before camped by nightfall.

It was satisfactory to find no traces of blacks. Bendigo now assumed a great air of importance. Paul and Harry agreed that he fancied himself the leader of the party. "Let him do so," said Paul, "it may make him more careful. He will consider himself responsible should we meet with any misfortune."

Travelling through a new country, hitherto untrod by the foot of a white man, is no doubt very interesting in theory, but it becomes dreadfully wearisome in practice. To go on hour after hour with huge gum-trees on every side, the only change being the sight of a kangaroo, a wallaby, a bandicoot, or a jolly little paddy-melon hopping away.

CHAPTER XV.

 TWO days had passed away; the young explorers made good progress. They now discovered, what caused them some anxiety, that they were running short of ammunition. Without it they would have a difficulty in obtaining food, although Bendigo and Bruce might help them. It was absolutely necessary to retain sufficient powder to protect themselves should they encounter any hostile blacks. Paul insisted that they should not fire another shot, except to kill a kangaroo or emu; at the same time, he did not wish to confess to Bendigo the small amount of ammunition they possessed. They had thus been for some time on short commons, and were beginning to feel the effects of scanty fare. Bendigo trapped several creatures, now and then catching a 'possum in its hole, or an iguana. Occasionally he found eggs where they themselves would not have discovered them. Had they been able to preserve the animals they caught they might have subsisted very well; but after a few hours, even though the meat was cooked, it became uneatable, and they were

obliged to give it to Bendigo or Bruce, who were not so particular.

They had been very unsuccessful all day, and had made a long march, when they encamped somewhat earlier than usual near a water-hole. They were fully aware of the risk they ran when selecting such a spot of a visit from the blacks; but they hoped, by keeping a good watch, not to be surprised by them. They knew that their chief danger would arise should they not be prepared ; for when the natives see white men on their guard, they will seldom venture to attack them. The fire had been lighted, but, excepting a 'possum and a few small eggs, and a little damper, they had nothing to eat. They had, however, a good supply of tea, the most welcome of beverages, the only one which can be taken with impunity under all circumstances.

An hour or more after dark was spent in talking over the prospects of their journey. In three or four days more they hoped to meet the captain's party.

Bendigo and Paul, accompanied by Bruce, having made a circuit of the camp, to be sure that no natives were lurking near, the whole party lay down to rest.

For the first time during their expedition, the following morning they started without breakfast, except a draught of cold water.

" I hope we shall find something during the day," said Harry. " This sort of work doesn't tend to keep up a fellow's spirits, and we shall be inclined to give a less favourable report of the country than it deserves."

As they rode along they carefully observed the character of the trees and soil over which they were passing. The grass was thicker and greener than they had anywhere seen it. Of course they kept an anxious look-out for game. They caught sight of kangaroos, wallabies, and other small animals in considerable numbers, but were unable to catch them, or even get near enough to shoot one.

Reggy now began to cry out bitterly for food. "People told us that this land was one flowing with milk and honey, we have had none of either since we started on this expedition," he exclaimed.

Just as he said this they observed Bendigo watching something in the air, and, urging on his horse, he started off ahead of them towards a large tree, beyond which they caught sight of the glitter of water. Near it were some trees with wide-spreading boughs, intertwined by numbers of the never-failing vine. Here was just the place they wanted.

Bendigo, knowing that they would camp there, dismounted, and hobbled his horse. They then saw him narrowly examining a tall gum-tree, up to which he had ridden. It must have been a hundred feet in height before any branches were reached.

"If he sees anything up there it will be of little use," observed Reggy, "for I am sure he will never get it."

"Stay a minute," answered Harry; "the black knows what he is about."

Bendigo, without explaining his object, cut some long vines; he then rapidly plaited, from the grass growing near, a rough basket, which he fastened to his belt. Taking the vines, he now twisted them in the form of a hoop round the tree, leaving sufficient space to admit his own body between the trunk and the hoop; holding the hoop in both hands, he jerked the side furthest from himself upwards. He then cut with his hatchet a notch for his feet, and then gave another jerk, and cut another notch, and thus up he went until he reached the branch.

The boys had never seen their black companion perform this feat before, and felt no little fear that he might slip down. It was wonderful with what rapidity he went

up, evidently feeling himself perfectly secure. In a few
minutes he returned, having cut a large comb of honey
out of a hole high up in the tree, the owners of which
were seen hovering about their rifled abode. Having
descended, he handed his prize to Paul, who, placing it
on a slip of bark, which served as a dish, served it on
leaves to his companions, with whom he shared it.

Without waiting to be complimented for his performance, of which he seemed to think nothing, the
black again started off, and ascended another tree,
towards which his quick eye had detected some bees flying.

The young explorers, who had eaten nothing for some
hours, set to with a will, and quickly devoured the first
comb, wax and all, being ready for the second, which
Bendigo soon brought them. He again came back with
a third, which, however, they could not attack, so he ate
the greater portion himself, giving the remainder to Bruce,
who gobbled it up with evident satisfaction.

"Plenty of food now," said Bendigo, as he led his companions from tree to tree, some of which were oaks, and
others honeysuckles. Wherever there was a hole in the
trunk it was occupied by a colony of bees. The insect
which makes this honey is exactly like a common house-
fly in appearance, the combs being generally small and
the wax quite black. The cells into which the comb is
divided are two or three times larger than those of the
English bee, and are roundish and irregular in shape,
but the honey is very good, being sweet, and having
besides a slight pleasantly acid taste. As these bees
possessed no sting, they could be robbed with impunity of
the result of their industry. Since that time English
bees have swarmed in prodigious numbers over the country,
and now afford ample food to whites and blacks alike.

"While we can get this honey there is no fear of
starving," observed Paul.

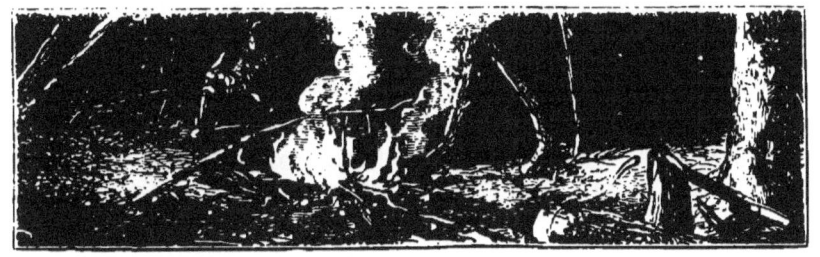

CHAPTER XVI.

THE young explorers had been upwards of two days travelling through a splendid country, subsisting chiefly on honey, though they might have revelled in abundance had they ventured to use their guns, when they came in sight of a river of veritable running water, bright and clear. In the distance, moreover, were a range of hills of no great elevation, but rising precipitously apparently out of the plain. Not without some difficulty they found a ford, by which they crossed the river. It ran south for some distance, then circled round in front of the hills, and then again struck off south and east. They galloped forward, eager to ascertain the character of the hills, for much depended on their being precipitous or not. Paul surveyed the country with a delighted eye.

"If cattle cannot get over these hills, we have found such a situation as we might look for over hundreds of miles and not find," he exclaimed; "they form a fence along one side and a half of the run, and the river, which appears to be impassable, except in a few places, will serve for another side and a half, or more, so that there will be but one outlet for cattle."

"Excellent!" cried Harry. "Father will be as pleased as you are if it turns out as we hope."

As they approached the hills they discovered, to their intense satisfaction, that they were as precipitous as they had expected. Cliffs from fifty to a hundred feet extended along the whole length of the range, with here and there dark impassable gullies, having steep sides, up which no cattle could climb. Down them ran streams of various sizes, all concentrating in the river through which they had passed.

"No fear of drought here!" exclaimed Paul. "It is worth all the trouble we have gone through to find it."

Returning to the river, they rode along, tracing it as far up as the range, which extended a considerable way to the southward, and would serve as a fence to their station. The country on the other side, further to the south, was more thickly wooded, and consequently afforded less pasture. There was a risk, to be sure, that the river might overflow, but they could find no traces of a flood. All would depend on the place where it took its rise; if in the range above them, there was no fear, but if it had a long course on the opposite side of the range, a sudden downpour of rain might swell its waters before they had time to escape through their natural channel. That important point would be ascertained when their father arrived. They had, it should be said, notched the trees as they came along, so that he was not likely to cross their track.

" In case there is a chance of the country being flooded, I think we might build our house on yonder knoll, close under the hill, with the river bending round it," observed Paul; "it is a beautiful spot, and we should get a fine view from it over the whole district. I vote that we camp there to-night, and set up a flag-staff, so that our father may see it miles off ; for I feel sure he will not pass to the west of this range without first examining the country where we now are."

Paul's proposal was at once adopted. The trees on the knoll, though growing pretty thickly, were of no great height, and it would be easy to cut a flag-staff long enough to rise above them.

" Old Bolter " was hobbled as usual, and the young explorers, having ascertained that the river was nowhere fordable in the neighbourhood of the knoll, nor up to the point where it came out of the hills, the rest of the horses were turned loose, as there was no fear of their bolting.

As they hoped their journey westward was now terminated, they ventured to shoot as many parrots and pigeons as would serve them for an ample meal. This done, they lighted their fire, leaving Reggy to cook the birds, while Paul, Harry, and Bendigo went down to the scrub on the bank of the river to cut a pine suitable for a flag-staff. The soft wood yielded easily to their axes, and in a few minutes it lay on the ground. To lop off the branches and bark it occupied but a short time, and then, all three placing it on their shoulders, they carried it up the hill.

" But what are we to do for a flag ? " asked Reggy.

" We must fasten our handkerchiefs and my spare shirt together. A strong breeze will be required, to be sure, to blow it out ; but, depend upon it, our father will guess what it means at any distance," answered Paul.

The flag was made, and lashed on with some strips of hide taken from the last kangaroo they had shot, as they had no halyards with which to hoist it. The pole was lashed to the trunk of another tree. When it was up, it was seen to tower above all those on the knoll. They enjoyed a better meal than they had had for many a day, and drank success to their new

"THEY CARRIED IT UP THE HILL"—(*See* p. 123).

station—for they already considered it their own—in pannikins of tea.

While daylight lasted they kept a look-out for the captain and his party; but their friends did not appear. As far as they could ascertain, no white man had ever before set foot in that region, and very proud they felt at being the discoverers of so fine a country. Below them they could just distinguish their horses feeding quietly, and they felt sure that the animals would not stray far from the camp.

Near the top of the knoll, on the steepest side, just behind their camp, was a huge rock, like an excrescence, although the rest of the elevation was almost smooth. As the glare of their fire fell on it at nightfall, it looked like the ruins of an ancient castle perched on the hillside.

" I vote we call this ' Castle Hill ; ' it will be a good name for our station," said Harry.

Paul and Reggy tried to find another name, but could not improve on Harry's suggestion. At length, as they were all pretty well tired with their day's work, they lay down by the fireside, wrapped in their blankets, Bruce keeping watch.

Two or three times during the night Paul was awakened by hearing the dog utter a low growling bark. On each occasion Bendigo started up, and looked out, but did not like to go far in the dark by himself. Paul asked him if he thought any one was near.

" Me see in morning," was the only answer he could obtain ; and the black crouched down again, as if going to sleep.

Paul, confident that Bruce—who was evidently on the alert—would arouse him should danger be near, again fell asleep. He did not awake Harry and Reggy, who slept on, notwithstanding Bruce's barking and his conversation with Bendigo. The black roused up Paul at daybreak.

" Stay here ; me go look round. Black fellows near, I tinkee."

Harry and Reggy soon got up, and shook themselves— the only dressing operation they had to perform.

" I vote we go down and have a bathe," exclaimed Harry.

" You had better not," said Paul. " Bendigo suspects

that natives have been near us during the night; and I believe that such was the cause of Bruce's barking. We must look to our arms, at all events, in case they should prove unfriendly. Not to lose time, let us light the fire and cook breakfast."

They all, accordingly set about doing so. As the light increased, Paul climbed to the rock which has been spoken of, to look out for the horses ; for he naturally feared that, if the blacks had been in the neighbourhood, they might have driven them away or speared them.

As he cast his eye over the plain he could nowhere see the animals. They might, of course, have got round to the other side of the knoll, but still their non-appearance made him anxious. A shout from Harry, announcing breakfast, called him back to the camp. Bendigo had not yet returned. It was not necessary to wait for him. The young explorers made a hearty meal—Bruce coming in for his share—to prepare them for the work to be done, whatever that might be.

They had just finished breakfast, having laid aside a share for the black, when he was seen coming up the hill, stealing among the bushes. He shook his head, as he sat down and gobbled up his breakfast.

"Black fellows here—no good—come again; horses gone too," and he pointed to the north-east, the only outlet to the region, except by a ford over the river.

"We must go after the horses at once, then," exclaimed Harry.

"No, I certainly would not," answered Paul; "our best plan will be to remain where we are until we can learn what the blacks are about. Should they attack us, we could not have a better place for defence than the one we occupy. If we find that they have driven off the horses, we might follow and try to recover them; but if not, I again say we should remain where we are."

Reggy thought Paul's plan the best, and Harry soon saw its wisdom. Bendigo also approved of it, and said that he would set out again and try to discover the whereabouts of the black fellows.

"There appear to be a good many birds on the knoll. We shall probably find some 'possums and other animals, so that we shall not want for food if we can catch them; but we must not throw a shot away," observed Paul. "We shall want our powder to keep the blacks in check."

Bendigo told them not to be anxious about food, as he could obtain as much for them as they could require. Having taken a survey round from the top of the rock, he glided down the knoll, keeping among the bushes so as not to be seen by any enemies who might be on the watch.

Although the three lads kept looking round on every side, they could nowhere discover him. Harry suggested that they should fortify their rock with small trees and boughs, which they could easily cut down, and which would keep off the spears of the natives.

"A very good idea," said Paul; and they all three set to work, trusting to Bruce to give them timely notice should strangers approach. They chose only small trees, which quickly yielded to their axes, and they were thus soon enabled to form a breastwork on the only accessible side of the rock. Although it was not capable of withstanding a determined rush of the enemy, yet as long as their ammunition lasted the blacks were not likely to come to close quarters.

They had made some progress in the work, when Bruce suddenly rushed partly down the hill, uttering a loud bark. The lads instantly sprang behind the breastwork, ready for action; but directly afterwards Bruce came back, wagging his tail, and, almost following him, Bendigo appeared.

"Black fellows all about," he said, looking approvingly at the fortification, the object of which he at once understood. He told them that they need not expect an attack for some time, though he was certain that the black fellows would surround them should they venture down into the plain on foot.

"But how are we to get back our horses?" asked Reggy; "and if we do not get them back, how are we to return home?"

Bendigo said that he hoped to recover them, as they were not very far off.

"If he does not, we must make up our minds to trudge back on foot. It will be a long journey, but he will not let us want for food," said Harry.

Bendigo, faithful to his promise, again left them, and soon returned, bringing a 'possum and several combs of honey. He also filled their water-bottles; so that they had sufficient provisions to stand a siege of some hours, at all events. He had gone on a second expedition, when he was seen hurrying back up the hill.

"Black fellows come!" he exclaimed, as he sprang behind the breastwork.

The boys got their rifles ready.

"We must not fire unless the natives show a determination to attack us," observed Paul; "their blood will then be on their own heads if they do so. We must get Bendigo to tell them that we wish to be at peace; and that if they will bring back our horses we will part on friendly terms."

Paul explained to Bendigo what he wished. The black laughed, as if he did not consider there would be any use in attempting to come to terms with his countrymen but merely patted his rifle, as though he considered that it contained the best argument they could employ.

They waited for some minutes.

"THE ATTACK OF THE BLACKS"—(see p. 131).

k

"I don't think the blacks are coming at all," said Harry.

"Bruce seems of a different opinion," answered Paul.

The dog was stretching out his neck, and slowly creep-. ing forward; presently he gave a loud bark, and then bounded back into the fort. At the same instant the side of the hill below them appeared covered with black forms, who kept flitting in and out among the trees, making their way upwards. Bendigo shouted to them, but they only replied with loud and derisive cries and shrieks. They had evidently made up their minds to destroy the white men. Flourishing their spears, they leaped from behind their cover, and came springing up the hill.

"Must not we fire?" asked Harry.

"Wait; they may even yet think better of it," answered Paul.

A flight of spears came rattling against the breast-work; but, fortunately, from the distance at which they were hurled, they either flew over or fell against their fortification.

In return, the four rifles cracked at the same moment. So well were they aimed, that the same number of their assailants fell, and rolled over down the hill, the rest scampering back, in evident alarm, to seek for the nearest shelter.

The little garrison immediately reloaded. Though so many of the natives had been killed or wounded, they quickly regained their courage; and, having received a lesson, took care as they advanced not to expose themselves. It was some time before Paul again gave the order to fire. His bullet alone struck an enemy; the others glanced off against the trees. They all speedily reloaded, and were ready once more to fire before the blacks threw their spears, which flew against the rock, without wounding any of them, although they all had narrow escapes—Paul's hat was pierced, a spear grazed Harry's shoulder, and another flew close to Reggy's ear. Notwithstanding this, they took good aim, wounding two of the blacks, who—as they had done before—rushed down the hill.

"Reload! quick! quick!" cried Paul.

They all fired at the retreating enemy.

In the excitement of the moment Paul had forgotten the necessity of husbanding their ammunition. On examining their powder, they found that they had not two rounds apiece left.

In spite of the loss of their companions—two, if not three, of whom had been killed outright—the blacks, after a short time, began again to mount the hill. Bendigo, without waiting for orders, fired, being instinctively followed by Harry and Reggy. Not one of the shots, however, took effect; and, with shouts and shrieks, the blacks came on.

CHAPTER XVII.

"HARRY and Reggy, we must sell our lives dearly," exclaimed Paul, as he prepared for a last desperate struggle with the blacks, who were infuriated at the loss of so many of their companions. The fact that they had not taken to flight showed that they were a fierce and warlike tribe, very different from most of those found in the southern parts of Australia. Harry had climbed to the higher part of the rock to take a look round.

"Hurrah!" he cried, "I see some horsemen coming across from the north-east, and driving some horses before them. They must be ours, and the people must be our father's party."

Paul and Reggy echoed Harry's shout. "We must not give in, whatever we do," said Paul, "we have our pistols loaded, and we must drive back the black fellows with them. Don't either of you miss your aim. We must not fire until they are close upon us. As soon as they come near enough I'll give their chief, if they've got one, the contents of my rifle, and that will, perhaps, check them."

Harry had still kept his post at the top of the rock, and taking off his jacket he waved it, pointing to the flag which flew just above them, while he shouted with all his might, forgetting, in the excitement, that the horsemen were too far off to hear him. His action, however, attracted the attention of the blacks, and they, looking round, discovered the horsemen. They immediately halted, and began jabbering away in loud voices. It was evident that they were alarmed at the sight of the strangers.

If three lads and a black had been able to hold them in check for so long a time, what chance would they have when encountered by a party of well-armed men on horseback ?

Such, probably, was the tenor of their remarks to each other. Notwithstanding this their chief endeavoured to lead them up the hill, apparently hoping to capture the fort before the arrival of the horsemen. He was flourishing his spear and shouting to his companions to come on, when he got within range of Paul's rifle.

"It is his own fault," said Paul, taking aim. His bullet struck the right shoulder of the savage, who went spinning round down the hill, and was soon in the midst of his followers, who now took to flight helter-skelter, and were soon lost to sight among the trees.

Bendigo proposed sallying out and killing some more of them, but Paul ordered him to remain quiet.

"We will hold our position until the white men come up," he said. "Harry, do you think they are our father's party ? "

"No doubt about it," answered Harry.

The defenders again raised a loud shout. This time they were heard, and, the captain leading, they were all soon mounting the hill. All that had occurred was briefly told. The captain had observed the beautiful run from the hill, and, fortunately turning back, had descended, and found the only entrance which existed. He had seen the flag in the distance, and guessing by whom it was hoisted, was making his way towards it.

He at once saw the necessity of teaching the blacks a lesson, and the horses he had recovered being saddled, the whole party set off in pursuit. The blacks, however, had got the start of them, and swam the river, having left their wives and children on the other side.

"I trust they have received a lesson they will not easily forget, and that when we come here, as I hope to do, they will not venture to attack us," said the captain.

Paul and Harry were delighted at hearing that their father had resolved to apply for the run. As no one else was likely to have made a claim for it, there was every probability that it would be granted to him. They were much surprised at the altered appearance and manners of Hector, whose cheek was well browned, and who looked infinitely more manly and fit for work than he had done before. He seemed in good spirits and greatly to have enjoyed the trip. Indeed, as they sat round the camp fire that evening, not a grumble did he mutter.

The captain was, of course, grieved to hear of Mr. Hayward's illness, though he hoped that they should find him perfectly recovered on their return. The next morning Bendigo went out to ascertain whether the blacks had taken their departure, while the captain and his party rode round the proposed run to notch the trees and make other marks for identifying it. The whole day was thus occupied, and on their return Bendigo met them with the satisfactory intelligence that the blacks had gone off to a distance, carrying their dead with them. It was a sign that they did not intend to come back.

The following morning, after a good night's rest, the

whole party commenced their journey homewards. The captain, having been very sparing of his ammunition had sufficient to enable them to obtain food, though, during two or three days they were somewhat hard put to it for water. The hole in which they found the dead cattle contained a sufficient supply for the horses and Bruce, but none of the rest of the party, except Bendigo, felt inclined to taste it.

They found Mr. Hayward quite recovered. The shepherds had treated him with all the attention they possibly could. The captain had warned his party not to speak of the new run in the presence of the shepherds, lest they might mention it to their employers, and create some dispute.

Stopping on Sunday to rest, they travelled on for the remainder of the week, performing nearly thirty miles a day, the horses all the time obtaining no other food than the grass they could pick up, and often having to go several hours without water; still they and their riders got back to Stratton in very good condition.

The captain had, without loss of time, to go to Brisbane to obtain legal possession of his new run. As soon as possible after his return, he intended to set out with his flocks, herds, and his family for the site of the new station.

The children, in consequence of the out-door life they led, had got into somewhat erratic ways. Miss Saville had done her best to teach the younger girls, as well as Tommy and Albert, but even they were apt to break loose and to rebel against her authority, as well as that of their elder sisters.

The season of wild fruit had come round, and raspberries were especially plentiful. Rob and Edgar determined that they must go off to the scrub to obtain a supply for preserving, and Tommy and Albert insisted on accompanying them.

"I go too," said Effie; "if we cannot reach the fruit high up, we can pick that growing near the ground as fast as you can."

Without asking leave they all set off, having first provided themselves with large baskets which Rob and Edgar had been busy in manufacturing.

They would certainly not have been allowed to go without Betty, but she was watching over little Sybil, who was unwell, and was not aware that they had set out. They went along to the westward on the edge of the scrub which the flood had not reached—indeed, its traces had even disappeared from the surface which it had covered. They were somewhat disappointed at first in not finding fruit in the abundance they had expected, and so they went on and on until they reached a part of the scrub sufficiently open to enable them to penetrate into it. Here Rob and Edgar thought that they could without difficulty procure plenty of fruit. They were soon hard at work picking away with great delight.

"Keep together," cried Rob, "or we may chance to lose ourselves."

"No fear," answered Effie, "we will look where you go."

Edgar said the same. Rob felt very proud of being the leader of so large a party, but in his eagerness to pick a quantity of fruit, he did not watch over them as carefully as he should have done. On and on they went, Rob making a remark every now and then to those near him. Presently he heard Tommy shriek out, "A snake, a snake!" and throwing down his basket, he ran off towards the more open part of the scrub.

"Come back!" cried Rob. "It is only a paddy-melon, and won't hurt you or any one else."

Tommy, however, would not stop.

"Come along, Edgar, and catch the child," cried Rob, forgetting Effie and Albert, whom he had not seen for some minutes.

It was some time before Tommy could be overtaken.

"You stupid monkey!" cried Rob, when he caught him; "there are no snakes here to do you any harm."

Tommy, however, was not easily persuaded, and still asserted that he had seen the head of a big snake. At length they got him to come back and pick up his basket.

"Hulloa! Where are Effie and Albert?" asked Rob. "We left them close here, I am sure."

They looked about in every direction; they shouted, but no answer came.

"This is provoking!" cried Rob. "I expected those children to keep close to us; see how obstinate they are! I'll make them remember this when we catch them."

Rob became very anxious when, after hunting about for some time, he could find neither his little sister nor his cousin. How they could have got out of hearing seemed incredible. Rob, though very clever in his own opinion, was in a serious difficulty. While he fancied that he was going west, he had turned east; and thinking that he was just getting out of the scrub, he found himself, to his surprise, close to the river.

His first exclamation was, "Dear me! how could we have got over to the other side?" Then, after due reflection, he recollected that was impossible; he must have gone in an opposite way to what he had supposed.

Darkness came on. Tommy began to cry, and Edgar felt very much inclined to join him. "Poor Albert! poor Effie! Where can they have gone?" They were a long way from home, they knew; but they dreaded going back without their little brother and sister. Indeed, in the dark they would be unable to find their way, for they had no notion of steering themselves by the stars. The fruit, though very fit for making jelly, was full of seeds, and not satisfying; but they had no other food, so at last they sat down and ate enough to allay the cravings of hunger.

The alarm at Stratton became very great when the children did not return. No one knew in what direction they had gone, but the baskets they had made had disappeared; consequently, it was supposed that they had set off on an expedition to pick fruit. At that hour it was impossible to see their trail; even Betty could not do it. However, Mr. Hayward, accompanied by the boys and Bruce, at once started in search of the missing children. They made their way along the edge of the scrub, and penetrated into it whenever they could find an opening, cooing at the top of their voices, and shouting loudly, "Rob, Tommy, Effie, Albert! answer! Where are you?"

No answer came.

"I trust that the black fellows have not got hold of them," said Mr. Hayward.

"We must pursue, and get them back," cried Harry. "Savage as the natives are, they would not dare to injure them."

Mr. Hayward did not reply; he might have known more of the natives than Harry did.

At length, having gone some distance, they heard a faint cooey in reply to theirs.

"Hurrah! That must be Rob's voice," exclaimed Harry; "though where it came from I cannot tell. I will cooey again."

Harry gave another loud cooey; again a distant answer was heard.

"Why, that must be behind us," said Harry; "it comes from the edge of the scrub."

They had by this time made their way into the interior. Bruce, on hearing the second cooey, pricked up his ears and bounded forward. They turned back, guided by Rob's voice, and casting the light of their lanterns about, they at length saw Rob standing up, with Tommy and Edgar lying down near him.

"Oh, I am so thankful you have come!" exclaimed Rob. "Have you found Effie and Albert?"

The question alarmed Mr. Hayward and the other boys "No; what has become of them?" asked Harry.

"We lost sight of them all of a sudden, and though we hunted about, we have not seen them since; and then we could not find our way home in the dark."

Mr. Hayward saw that there was no use in scolding poor Rob, who was already dreadfully alarmed, and fully conscious that he was to blame for the loss of the two children. Tommy and Edgar, who had dropped off soundly asleep from fatigue, were now awakened.

"I will continue the search for the other children," said Mr. Hayward, turning to the boys; "but the rest had better return with Rob and the little ones. If I do not soon come back with the children, follow in this direction in the morning with Bendigo and Betty, who will assist in tracing them out better than we can. Do not alarm your mothers more than is necessary, and assure them that I have little doubt but that we shall find the truants. I will take Bruce with me."

"Go, good dog—go!" said Harry, patting him on the head.

Bruce understood his duty, and without hesitation accompanied Mr. Hayward; while Harry and Reggy, taking charge of the children, made their way back to Stratton with the rest of the party, the younger ones every now and then sobbing as they thought of their carelessness in losing sight of Effie and Albert.

It is needless to describe the alarm which the disappearance of the two children caused their mothers and sisters. The elder boys were eager to set off again at once, but were persuaded to wait until daylight; when, accompanied by the two blacks, they immediately started off to commence a search for the lost children.

CHAPTER XVIII.

The Children recovered—Journey into the Interior—Arrival at Castle Hill—Station Established—House attacked by Natives—Conclusion.

POOR Mrs. Berrington's anxiety produced a succession of fainting fits ; she therefore required the constant attention of her sister and Mrs. Hugh, who was herself much alarmed at the disappearance of the children. As soon as the girls had performed the necessary duties of the morning, they all set out in the direction taken by their brothers, carrying with them a supply of food, as the party, which had started early in the morning, had gone away without breakfast.

It was noon before the girls heard the cooeys uttered by the searching-party, which proved that the children had not yet been discovered.

Hurrying along, they at last came in sight of Reggy, who was at the very edge of the scrub.

" Have you seen anything of them ? " asked Mary.

" Nothing : nor of Mr. Hayward either," was the unsatisfactory answer.

Poor Mary's heart sank. She dearly loved little Effie, and his sisters in their way were very fond of Albert; besides, they believed that it would be the death of their mother if he were lost.

Reggy gave notice to the rest of the party, when they were within hail, that the ladies had arrived with some provisions; and although they all declared that they were too anxious to be hungry, they not unwillingly partook of the food the thoughtful girls had brought with them.

Once more they resumed their search; but as hour after hour went by, and neither the children nor Mr. Hayward were found, the anxiety of the searching-party became almost unbearable. To abandon the search was not to be thought of. Bendigo and Betty had not hitherto discovered the trail, for in so thick a wood, it was no easy matter, even for them.

At length they shouted out, "We have the trail! we have the trail!" and, like two beagles, off they set, with their noses close to the ground.

The excitement of the party may be supposed. The boys managed to follow as quickly as they could, though their clothes were nearly torn from their backs. The rest of the party remained outside the scrub, keeping up a communication with those within. The day, however, was wearing on, and no sign of the children had yet been seen. The sun's rays, as he sank towards the west, were glancing almost horizontally through the trees, when a bark was heard. Paul gave a loud cooey. It was answered, and greatly to their joy they saw Mr. Hayward coming along with the children in his arms. The blacks had only just before discovered him seated on the ground, and feeding them with some pigeon which he had shot and some wild fruit he had collected.

Mary took Effie in her arms, Paul carried Albert on his shoulders, thus relieving Mr. Hayward, who was pretty well worn out. He had gone on all the previous night, and greater part of that morning, keeping up with Bruce, who had been running before him, until he was nearly exhausted. Suddenly Bruce, with a loud bark, bounded forward, and to his great joy he discovered the children, who had evidently cried themselves to sleep. On being awakened by the dog, the first thing they did was to ask for food, which it had taken some time to obtain.

It was late at night before they got back, when they found Captain Berrington, and the anxiety which the news he had received on his arrival had caused was soon brought to an end. He had secured the run, and wished immediately to set out to take possession of it. He expected the drays soon to arrive with the various stores and provisions he had purchased. The elder ladies, Mrs. Berrington especially, looked forward with some alarm to this journey; although Mrs. Hugh did not express her feelings. Aunt Emily and the girls were, however, in good spirits, and expected to enjoy it.

At last the preparations were completed. Three drays, each drawn by four horses, to carry the ladies and children, were covered over and fitted up internally as comfortably as circumstances would allow. The other drays, laden with stores, were to be drawn by oxen. Reggy and Hector rode on horseback, as they would assist in the arduous task of driving the cattle. The captain, Mr. Berrington, and Mr. Hayward drove the three drays, while Paul and Sandy—with the assistance of three shepherds and hut-keepers—took charge of the sheep. There were three spare saddle-horses that the young ladies might ride whenever they wished. Thus arranged, they started early in the morning.

When the party moved forward, they had the appearance of a large tribe migrating. The long line of drays, with the herds of cattle, the drove of horses and flocks of sheep, with their numerous attendants, some mounted, others on foot; the oxen lowing, the sheep bleating, the shouts of the drivers, and the stockmen's whips sounding above all. The huge drays were each dragged by twelve bullocks, the two polers and leaders being steady old stagers, as were those immediately in front of the polers.

Thus they moved forward, resting only on Sunday. The most difficult part of their journey was surmounting the range, when even Mrs. Berrington preferred climbing up on foot to remaining in the dray. The bright fresh air, and the necessity of exerting herself, seemed to do her good; and by the time she reached the top, though somewhat fatigued, she appeared a different person, being not a little proud of her performance. Even the warmest admirers of the country, however, had to confess that there was a great sameness in the scenery, and many of the rivers and creeks they crossed had no water in them.

An ample supply of water was carried in the drays for the use of the travellers; but often the horses, cattle, and sheep suffered greatly from having to go a long way before a stream or a water-hole could be reached.

The gentlemen's guns amply supplied the larder, so that it was necessary only occasionally to kill a sheep, or one of the oxen.

"There's 'Castle Hill,' mother!" cried Harry, riding up to the dray in which Mrs. Hugh and some of the girls were seated—pointing as he spoke to the knoll which he and his companions had so bravely defended against the blacks, and which could be seen below the range bounding the plain on the west.

The whole party pushed forward, and by evening were encamped at the foot of the knoll. Every one was delighted with the situation, while they felt sure the

climate was superior to that of Stratton, although the
soil might not produce the tropical fruits which flourished
nearer the coast. No time was lost in preparing the
ground on which to build the house. To level this
sufficiently for the purpose required two or three days'
hard work, but everybody set to with a will. The house
was to face south, overlooking a long stretch of the river,
and a boundless plain beyond, with a view of the picturesque hill on the right.

We must not describe the house building, every one being engaged in it, except the men absolutely required to herd
the cattle and sheep, and that was comparatively an easy
task. Only one outlet required watching, and the animals
were not inclined to stray from the rich pasture on which
they found themselves. The blacks and dingoes had of
course to be looked after; but Bendigo reported that there
were none of the former in the neighbourhood, although
it was impossible to say at what time they might appear.

The house, when completed, was far larger than Stratton,
and easily held the two families; while, according to the
captain's design, wings could be put up on either side for
the accommodation of any fresh comers.

Stock-yards and cattle-pens had then to be formed, the
latter close to the river, where the sheep, before shearing,
could be washed, a very important process.

The station being a large one, the gentlemen were often
on horseback from morning until night, going round to
the different runs. The huts were put up in various
directions for the accommodation of the stockmen and
shepherds; in some instances in imitation of Castle Hill,
or with small gardens near them, very unusual, it must
be owned, in that part of Australia.

On an Australian farm work never ceases, but at certain seasons there is less than at other times, and on these
occasions pleasant excursions were made on horseback in

various directions by the younger members of the family.

A party had been formed to visit a waterfall farther off than they had yet ridden. Paul, Harry, and Reginald escorted Mary, Lizzie and Gertrude, while Miss Saville, Janet, and Adela remained at home. Mr. Hayward had gone out emu shooting, while the captain and Mr. Berrington had started off to visit a station at some distance. Janet and Adela were seated at their work in the verandah in front of the house, when Albert, who was playing in the shade near them, exclaimed, " See ! what can those black things be floating in the river ? "

" They must be fish," said Effie.

" Fish ! No, they are round and black."

Janet looked out. She, too, could distinguish some black objects. The captain's spy-glass hung in the hall. Getting it she saw at once that the black objects were the heads of natives. They quickly came to the shore and began crawling along towards the house. There were a considerable number, armed with spears and clubs. In another minute they would have landed and have escaped her observation, had not it been drawn to them by Albert's exclamation. They could be coming with no good intent. All the gentlemen were away. To obtain assistance in time was impossible. The blacks might attack and pillage the house, and be off again, before any of the party could return. Sandy, and perhaps another man, might be in the stock-yard near the hill, but how to summon them in time was the question.

Janet called Rob, who, with Edgar, was in the carpenter's shop at the back of the house.

Rob at once volunteered to go down and try and find Sandy. She charged him to be careful to keep out of the view of the savages. The first thing to be done was to shut the doors and windows. Adela and Edgar at once began to do so, while Janet hurried in to tell her mother, and aunt, and Miss Saville. The latter immediately assisted in preparing the house for defence.

Though the savages, if they intended an attack, might ultimately force their way in, it would take some time to tear down the shutters, which were secured by strong bars. The ladies were looking out eagerly for the return of Rob with Sandy. Scarcely had all the doors and windows been made fast, than the natives appeared hurrying up the hill with their spears and clubs in hand.

" What arms have we got ? " asked Miss Saville. " We must use them and fight to the last, sooner than yield."

They found two rifles and three brace of pistols.

" Can you load them ? " inquired Miss Saville.

" I have seen my brothers very often do so, and mamma can, but we will not call her until it is necessary, she is attending to Aunt Augusta, who is in a dreadful state of alarm."

" But where is the powder ? "

" Here is a powder flask," cried Edgar, " but, dear me ! there's nothing in it."

In vain they searched about. No one could tell where the captain kept the powder. It was in a safe place, that they knew, and he was certain to have a store in the house, probably in some spot from whence he could easily remove it in case of fire.

" The blacks have evidently been watching the house, and have seen all the gentlemen go away," observed Miss Saville. " If we could fire a few shots at them, they would fancy that some of our friends have returned, and would probably take to flight."

They hunted round and round; even Mrs. Hugh could not tell where the powder was to be found. Not a moment was to be lost, and already the blacks were almost at the top of the hill. Up they came, about a hundred of them. Probably they were those who had attacked Paul and had been so signally defeated. They had now come to revenge themselves in a terrible way. The girls could hear them approaching. They halted for an instant on finding the doors and windows closed, and were consulting together. They were evidently disappointed, having expected to surprise the house. At any moment a fire might be opened on them. Finding, however, that they were allowed to remain with impunity in front of the house, a party of them rushed up to the door and began battering away with their clubs, hoping to break it open. In addition to the bars, the girls had placed the dining-room table and the heaviest articles of furniture they could find against it.

" If they break in we must run for refuge to mamma's room, and barricade the door as well as we can. We may delay them, at all events. Oh! if we had but a charge of powder, one single shot might frighten the savages."

All this time the search was continued for powder, but with the same want of success. Already the door was giving way. It was strong and heavy, being formed of thick slabs fastened to cross-pieces. First one slab was broken and beaten in, then another, and the blacks began to thrust through the hole with their spears.

"We must fly !" cried Miss Saville, taking Effie and Sybil. "Do, Janet, do, Adela—come, come; do not venture to remain here longer. Run, Edgar and Albert! the savages will kill you if you remain."

" I will show them the muzzle of this rifle; it may keep them in check for a few moments longer," exclaimed Janet. Taking the weapon, she thrust it through the gap made by the blacks' clubs.

It had the effect Janet expected. Once more they retreated, but finding that no shot was fired, the savages again came on. Blow after blow resounded on the door, the splinters flew about, when with a loud crash the door gave way. Two or three savages were on the point of springing in, when a rifle-shot was heard, and one of them fell ; the next instant Janet, who was the last to leave the spot, saw Mr. Hayward spring forward and with the butt of his rifle strike down two more. What was her alarm, however, to find that instead of flying, the rest were attacking him with their clubs, the blows of which he could with difficulty parry. Still he bravely kept his post in the verandah, preventing the blacks from again stepping on to it.

Several minutes he waged the unequal fight, keeping the blacks at bay. Already he had been struck more than once ; his strength must fail at last. Some savages farther off, finding that the clubs of those in front were of no avail, rushed forward with their spears, and in another instant they would have pierced the white man, when a couple of shots laid two of them low. The shots were followed by the appearance of Rob, Sandy, and Jock Andrews, one of the men, who furiously threw themselves on the savages, Rob firing his pistol at the head of one of them. The blacks, not knowing how many white men might be following, took to flight and rushed down the hill, allowing Mr. Hayward and the rest time to reload. Janet, from behind the fragments of the door, handed out the two rifles, which Sandy and his companion loaded and as quickly discharged at the flying enemy, whom they then pursued down the hill, uttering loud shouts, in which they were joined by Bruce's fierce bark, he having at that instant been attracted to the spot.

The blacks made straight for the river, into which they plunged and swam across, without even looking behind them ; nor did they stop on landing, but made direct for the " bush." To follow them would have been useless with so small a party.

Mr. Hayward was anxious to get back, to ascertain if any of the ladies had been injured, and to repair the damage caused by the savages before the return of the party on horseback. There was some risk that the savages might fall in with the latter.

Brave little Rob offered to gallop off to warn them. Jock Andrews begged that he might go with Master Rob. There were still two horses in the paddock, though not very good ones. They were quickly caught and saddled, and Rob and his attendant set off. They had to cross by the ford some way down the river, in which direction the riding-party was coming. They would have to make a wide circuit, so as not to fall in with the blacks.

Rob and Jock rode on as fast as their sorry steeds would allow, looking out for the savages, who might, they feared, be on the watch for the riding party, to revenge themselves for the defeat they had suffered. They had gone some distance, when Jock exclaimed—

"There they are, Master Rob, there they are!"

"What, the blacks!" cried Rob. "We must keep clear of them, and gallop on."

"No, sir, the captain and the ladies," answered Jock, who, standing up in his stirrups, could obtain a wider view than his young companion.

"Hurrah!" cried Rob, and he dashed on to meet the party.

"What has happened, my lad?" exclaimed the captain in a tone of alarm, on seeing him approach.

Rob briefly explained what had happened.

"Thank heaven that they have escaped," said the captain. "We nearly fell in with the blacks, but seeing a mob of them in the distance, I thought it prudent to make a circuit, and so avoided them, or I don't know what would have been the consequences."

The captain was, of course, anxious to reach home.

The remainder of the distance was performed at a gallop. They found Mrs. Berrington greatly recovered, and Mrs. Hugh as calm as ever. Janet and Adela received their meed of praise. They had proved themselves true heroines, for had it not been for their courage and presence of mind—in all human probability the whole family would have been destroyed by the savage blacks.

Paul and Harry immediately volunteered to ride off and obtain the assistance of the police, lest the blacks —as it was probable they would do—might return.

While the lads were gone, the captain and his brother, with Mr. Hayward, the rest of the boys, and the men, employed themselves in repairing the door and further fortifying the house. Their labour was rendered unnecessary, however, by the arrival of a strong party of police, led by Paul and Harry, who had fortunately found them nearer than they had expected.

Chase was immediately made after the blacks, who were overtaken and severely punished for their unprovoked attack on Castle Hill Farm. Several were made prisoners, and the captain begged not only that their lives might be spared, but treated them so kindly that when set at liberty they expressed their regret at having attempted to injure so good a man, and promised that they and their tribe would henceforth be friends with the whites. Some [of them indeed came back, and, under Mr. Hayward's instruction, became so far civilized as to make themselves very useful, and two or three of their number imbibed the truths of Christianity.

Hector, greatly to his delight, obtained a commission as an officer in the police force; but he was very glad, after the experience of a year, to return to the farm, where, wonderful to relate, he ultimately became very useful. Captain Berrington and his family worked steadily on, and were rewarded for their industry by the success of most of their undertakings. They, of course, experienced the vicissitudes of settlers in general; but, though they occasionally lost many of their cattle and sheep, their flocks and herds increased, and were soon scattered far and wide over the surrounding country.

Putting their trust in God, and applying themselves diligently to the task they had undertaken, they were, on the whole, as successful as they could desire, and their cousins from England had every reason to be thankful that they had come out from the old country to become settlers in Australia.

THE END.

NEW TWO-SHILLING STORY BOOKS.

All Illustrated throughout, and containing Stories for Young People.

Crown 8vo, handsomely bound in cloth gilt.

Price 2s. each.

Little Flotsam. A Story for Boys and Girls: and other Tales. By ROBERT RICHARDSON, B.A., Author of "Phil's Champion," &c.

Madge and Her Friends, or Living unto Others. By MARY F. A. TENCH, Author of "Little Ned Mason, or the Beauty of Holiness," &c.

The Children of the Court, and Two Little Waifs. By F. MORELL HOLMES, Author of "Faith's Father,"&c.

The Four Cats of the Tippertons; and other Stories about Animals. By JULIA GODDARD, Author of "Worth More than Gold," &c.

Marion's Two Homes. By RUTH MITCHELL, Author of "Aunt Lucia's Locket," &c.

The Little Folks' Sunday Book. By CHRISTIAN REDFORD.

Two Fourpenny Bits. By the Author of "Tiny Houses."

Poor Nelly. By the Author of "Paws and Claws."

Tom Heriot. By EDWIN HODDER (Old Merry).

Through Peril to Fortune. By A. F. LIESCHING.

Aunt Tabitha's Waifs. By the Author of "Little Hinges."

In Mischief Again. By the Author of "Hugh's Heroism," "Nelly's Champion," &c.

Maid Marjory. By the Author of "Little Hinges."

NEW SERIES OF HALF-CROWN STORY BOOKS.

Crown 8vo, cloth gilt, 2s. 6d. each.

Little Empress Joan. By MADELINE BONAVIA HUNT, Author of "Little Hinges," &c. Illustrated throughout.

Adventures of Working Men. From the Note Book of a Working Surgeon. By G. MANVILLE FENN. Illustrated.

Golden Days. An English Girl's School Life in Germany. By JEANIE HERING. *New Edition.*

Notable Shipwrecks. Tales of Disaster and Heroism at Sea. By UNCLE HARDY. Illustrated. *New Edition.*

The Wonders of Common Things. By ANNIE CAREY. Being a New Edition, in One Vol., of "Autobiography of a Lump of Coal," &c., and "Threads of Knowledge." Illustrated.

Friends I have Made. By G. MANVILLE FENN. Illustrated.

CASSELL'S ONE-SYLLABLE SERIES.

Each Book containing Eight Coloured Illustrations, and bound in cloth, gilt edges.

Price 2s. 6d. each.

Æsop's Fables.
Sandford and Merton.

Reynard the Fox.
The Pilgrim's Progress.

Evenings at Home.

CASSELL'S CHILDREN'S TREASURIES.

A Series of Picture Books for Children, uniform in size and price, each containing 43 Full-page Pictures and accompanying Stories, Poetry, or Music. Square crown 8vo, cloth, 1s. each.

Simple Rhymes for Happy Times.

Tuneful Lays for Merry Days.

Cheerful Songs for Young Folks.

Pretty Poems for Young People.

The Children's Joy.

Pretty Pictures and Pleasant Stories.

Our Picture Book.

Tales for the Little Ones.

My Sunday Book of Pictures.

Sunday Garland of Pictures and Stories.

Sunday Readings for Little Folks.

CASSELL'S CHILDREN'S LIBRARY.

All Illustrated, and bound in cloth, gilt edges.

Price 3s. 6d. each.

The Children's Album. Containing nearly 200 Engravings, with Short Stories by UNCLE JOHN. 368 pages, cloth gilt.

Children's Sunday Album, The. By the Author of "A Trap to Catch a Sunbeam." With upwards of 150 Engravings.

Playing Trades. By HERACLITUS GREY. With Sixteen Illustrations printed in Colours.

The Story of Robin Hood. With Eight Coloured Plates.

The True Robinson Crusoes. A Series of Stirring Adventures. With Twenty Full-page Illustrations.

Off to Sea. A Story for Boys. By W. H. G. KINGSTON. With Eight Illustrations printed in Colours.

The Old Nursery Rhymes; or, The Merrie Heart. With Eight full-page Coloured Plates from Designs by WALTER CRANE, and 100 Illustrations.

THE COSY CORNER SERIES.

A Series of Story Books for Children. Each Book containing nearly ONE HUNDRED PICTURES. Fcap. 8vo, cloth gilt, gilt edges.

Price 2s. each.

See-saw Stories.

Little Chimes for All Times.

Wee Willie Winkie. By C. L. MATÉAUX.

Bright Sundays.

Pet's Posy of Pictures and Stories.

Dot's Story Book.

Story Flowers for Rainy Hours.

Little Talks with Little People.

Bright Rays for Dull Days.

Chats for Small Chatterers.

Pictures for Happy Hours.

Ups and Downs of a Donkey's Life.

BOOKS FOR GIRLS.

Heroines of the Mission Field. By Mrs. EMMA RAYMOND PITMAN, Illustrated throughout. 5s.

School Girls. By ANNIE CAREY. Cloth gilt, 5s.

Better than Good. A Story for Girls. With Four full-page Illustrations. By ANNIE E. RIDLEY. 5s.

Jane Austen and her Works. By SARAH TYTLER. With Steel Portrait and Steel Title. 5s.

Happy Little People. By OLIVE PATCH. Crown 4to, cloth, gilt
edges, with numerous Illustrations, price 5s.

Old Proverbs with New Pictures. With 64 fac-simile COLOURED
PLATES from Original designs by LIZZIE LAWSON. The Text by C. L. MATÉAUX.
Crown 4to, handsomely bound, 6s.

"My Diary." With 12 COLOURED PLATES and 366 SMALL WOODCUTS
by a new Artist, specially executed for the work ; together with blank space for every
day in the year for small mems. by small writers. In elegant binding, price 2s. 6d.

The Wonderland of Work. Being the "How and Why" of many
interesting things to be found therein. By C. L. MATÉAUX, Author of "Home
Chat." With numerous Original Illustrations. Extra crown 4to, 320 pages, 7s. 6d.

The Little Folks' Album of Music. Containing a charming
Collection of Music (with Words). Illustrated. Crown 4to, cloth, gilt edges, 3s. 6d.

Peter Parley's Annual. 41st Issue, containing a Series of Original
Stories. Illustrated with 9 COLOURED PLATES, printed in Oil, and 12 full-page
Engravings. Cloth, gilt edges, 5s.

Wild Adventures in Wild Places. By DR. GORDON STABLES.
Illustrated throughout. Crown 4to, cloth, gilt edges, 5s.

Familiar Friends. By OLIVE PATCH. Illustrated throughout.
168 pages, crown 4to, cloth gilt, 5s.

Tim Trumble's "Little Mother." By C. L. MATÉAUX. With
18 Illustrations by GIACOMELLI. 4to, cloth, gilt edges, 5s.

The Favourite Album of Fun and Fancy. Illustrated throughout
by ERNEST GRISET. Crown 4to, cloth, 3s. 6d.

Little Folks. The Half-Yearly Volumes. Each containing COLOURED
FRONTISPIECE and nearly 500 Pictures. Extra crown 4to, coloured boards, 3s. 6d. ;
cloth gilt, 5s. each. LITTLE FOLKS *is also published in Monthly Parts at 6d.*

Pictures to Paint. With numerous ORIGINAL COLOURED PLATES,
with accompanying Outline Engravings intended for Water-Colour Painting. In
coloured wrapper, 1s. ; or cloth gilt, 2s.

"Little Folks" Illuminating Book. Containing a Series of
Texts in Outline, with Coloured Copies for the guidance of Competitors. Price 1s. ;
or cloth gilt, 2s.

"Little Folks" Painting Book. A Series of Outline Illustrations by
KATE GREENAWAY, adapted for Water-Colour Painting, with Descriptive Stories
and Verses by G. WEATHERLY. Price 1s. ; cloth gilt, 2s.

"Little Folks" Black and White Painting Book. With Illustrations in Black and White, and Amusing Verses. 1s. ; or in cloth, 2s.

"Little Folks" Nature Painting Book. With numerous Illustra-
tions, intended for Water-Colour Painting, of well-known British Flowers, Butterflies,
Birds, and Animals. 1s. ; or cloth gilt, 2s.

Cassell, Petter, Galpin & Co.'s Complete Catalogue, containing a List of *Several Hundred Volumes,* including Bibles and
Religious Works, Fine-Art Volumes, *Children's Books, Dictionaries,
Educational Works, History, Natural History, Household* and *Domestic
Treatises, Handbooks* and *Guides, Science, Travels,* &c. &c., together
with a Synopsis of their numerous Illustrated Serial Publications,
sent post free on application to

CASSELL, PETTER, GALPIN & CO., Ludgate Hill, London.